SATED

JANE THORNTON, BOOK 3

C.E. BLACK

This is a work of fiction. Names, characters, places, and incidents either are the product of the author's imagination or are used fictitiously. Any resemblance to actual persons, living or dead, business establishments, events or locales is entirely coincidental.

SATED

ISBN-13: 978-0-9987885-9-3

Printed in the United States of America

PRAISE FOR HUNGER

"It's not your typical romance and it's not your typical zombie read. It's so much more!"
- My Book Obsession

"The passion between Jane and her two men is off the charts hot. There's lots of danger, fights, survival, and plenty of panty melting scenes in this first installment of CE Black's new series. I loved it and can't wait to see what happens next."
- Just One More Page

"This book was thrilling, dangerous, hot as f**k and just so...well, AMAZING!"
- Marie's Tempting Reads

"I always know that I am going to experience a story that is nothing short of spectacular, and this was no exception. Hunger tantalized all my appetites and left me starving for more."
- Author S.H. Timmins

JANE THORNTON TRILOGY
BY C.E. BLACK

"There's safety in pairs, but three is better."

HUNGER
STARVED
SATED

1

Sweat trickled down between my breasts, cooling the heated flesh before being caught by the stroke of a warm tongue. I couldn't stop the gasp from escaping my swollen lips, but when I shifted away from the touch, the man between my thighs took the hint. With a sigh, he pulled back, leaving me empty once more.

Sated, Kaden fell back onto the bed, his chest rising and falling rapidly from exertion as he watched me closely. Hiding from his stare, I swung my legs over the side of the bed, giving me some much-needed space. As annoying as it was, the slightest touch on my spine didn't surprise me. Kaden had never been a quitter.

Twisting away, I reached for the panties sitting at the foot of the bed, then stood in search for the rest of my clothes that were scattered across the room.

Kaden sighed. "Jane, we can't keep going like this. You have to talk to me."

I can't talk, remember? Knowing my sarcasm wouldn't be appreciated, I kept the thought to myself.

"Will you ever forgive me?" he asked.

I stiffened at the soft tone of his voice. The pleading, vulnerable undercurrents were unlike Kaden. Except when it came to the subject of his leaving and my forgiveness. I'd fallen for it weeks before. And I couldn't deny the fluttering in my belly even now. But I straightened my spine and shook my head, unable to communicate my feelings. I thought I had forgiven him— them. But now… I wasn't sure I could trust him to stick around. Mason hadn't.

Dressed, I turned for the door, pausing when the weight of Kaden's stare caused the back of my neck to tingle. After a deep breath, I looked back, making eye contact for the first time since our hormones had taken over, and we'd fallen onto the bed in a tangle of arms and legs. A shiver crept up my spine. The pleading gaze I'd expected to see was absent, replaced by a cold stare I hadn't seen from him in a long time.

"Where are you going?" he asked in a voice as firm as his expression.

The question was more of a demand, and if it had come from anyone else, or if the circumstances had been different, I wouldn't have answered.

"Supply run," I signed.

Finding an abandoned house to stay in hadn't been difficult. This one was pretty nice. The linens in the closet had been clean and there'd been no dead bodies left behind. Both pluses in my book. But there hadn't been much food in the cabinets.

I was hoping we wouldn't have to stay there for long, though. We were only a couple miles east of the secret CDC facility, and hopefully, close to catching up with Mason. Thankfully, Kaden had remembered a conversation during his time with the military and had

had a good idea where they were heading with Mason. And, as it turned out, Aidan had a surprising talent for tracking.

In a fluid motion that was neither hurried or languid, Kaden rolled from the bed. My quiet gasp could not have been helped. Not when presented with the lean, nude body of the man I was in love with.

I eyed his face to find him watching me still. He didn't smirk or tease. He only saw. Saw how much I wanted him. How much I loved him… And how much I hated him for it.

His jaw twitched, a sign he was grinding his teeth again. Then he dropped his eyes and bent to retrieve his clothing. Though we'd been in a frenzy of lust, his clothes somehow had all landed in the same black pile at the end of the bed. I wondered about that. Not just his propensity toward neatness, but also his dark color choices. I would have asked him if he hadn't spoken.

"Take Annabelle with you." I started to nod when he ruined it by adding, "It's too dangerous for you to be out there alone."

Had I imagined the emphasis on the word you? As if I would be in more danger than any of the rest of us?

As he buttoned his pants, my raised brow went unnoticed. As did my exit. By the time I heard him call my name, I'd already grabbed my bag and was out the door. However, my plan to go off on my own was thwarted by the ever-cheerful Annabelle.

"Want company?" she asked.

The thought of telling her the truth, that no, I didn't want company, flitted across my mind, but I dismissed it just as fast. It would only raise her curiosity. Instead, I gave her a short nod as she fell into step beside me.

"Where's Poco?" I asked.

"Taking a nap with Aidan. The two of them are attached at the hip now," she said, her scowl telling me she wasn't too happy to have her dog befriend our ally.

"He needed the sleep," she continued, her frown deepening. "He stayed up all night while Aidan was on watch. Poor thing was pooped."

We approached the truck, and I took advantage of her distraction. *"I'm driving,"* I signed, jumping into the driver's seat.

The rear-view mirror caught Annabelle's eye roll, and I smiled as she climbed into the cab. "You're so going to pay for that," she said. "You know I hate your driving."

Right palm over my heart, I parted my lips in fake outrage.

"Yes, you," she grumbled.

"I am not a bad driver," I signed as I held out my hand for the keys.

With a shake of her head, she crossed her arms, refusing to hand them over. "You almost got me killed last time I rode with you."

That had been three days before, and the whole incident had not been my fault. Plus, the situation had nothing to do with my driving. I was sure she knew it too, but Annabelle had a knack for knowing when I needed cheering up. And I could admit I liked it when she tried. In fact, our banter was exactly what I needed right now to get mind off other things. And people.

"You wanted me to stop the car," I signed

"Yeah, because a horde of flesh-eaters crossed the road. I didn't mean we should jump out and fight them."

"Two flesh-eaters." I held up two fingers.

"More like twelve."

"Four."

"Eight."

I gave her a look, and she finally threw the keys at me. "Fine. There were five. Still! We could have died."

Shaking my head, I turned the ignition over and put the truck in drive. As silence settled inside the cab, my foot hesitated on the accelerator. With a sigh, I faced my friend, giving her serious, apologetic eyes.

When her gaze softened and the tense lines around her mouth disappeared, I removed my hands from the wheel and signed, *"Why did the flesh-eater cross the road?"*

Annabelle's brows furrowed, then with a huff, she rolled her eyes.

"Well? Why?" I asked. We wouldn't be going anywhere until she answered, and she knew it.

Annabelle threw her hands up. "I don't know, why?"

I pressed my foot lightly on the gas to get us moving as I answered, *"To eat the chicken, of course."*

Annabelle bit her lip but was unable to hold back her laughter. Smiling, I took us down the mountain. I had intended to take us into the closest town, but a sign for one of those high-priced neighborhoods caught my eye. Annabelle saw it too and pointed. I took the turn and slowed.

"Damn! These are mansions," Annabelle exclaimed softly, her voice filled with awe.

I wouldn't have considered the two and three-story brick homes mansions, but by the size of them, they weren't far off from her description.

"I hope we find some decent clothes," Annabelle remarked as I pulled the truck to the side of the single lane road. "I'm getting desperate."

Me too, I thought, fingering one of the many holes in

5

my shirt. Food, clothes, and weapons. That was the gist of our shopping list. Oh, and hygiene products. I would kill for a stick of deodorant.

Loaded with empty bags and our weapons, we went into the first house together and got lucky. A woman had lived there. Placing my bags on the bed, I stripped off my pants and tried on a pair of jeans. I didn't know much about designer clothing, but they looked expensive. I didn't care, as long as they were comfortable. The size was much smaller than I'd ever worn, so as they slid over my hips and buttoned easily, my brows rose in surprise. I'd lost more weight than I'd feared.

"Hey, those look wicked," Annabelle said as she walked into the room. "They make you look too skinny, though."

She went to the closet, yanking a pair of jeans off the hanger for herself. "By the way, I found a few cans in the kitchen, but not much," she said as she pulled off her pants and tried on the jeans. "Hey look, they fit."

She did a little turn and I nodded. *"We need more food,"* I signed.

"Agreed. We'll take a few pairs of these and some shirts if they fit. Oh, I see a couple of pairs of tennis shoes. I'd prefer boots though."

After packing what we could use, we continued on with our search. A few bags of clothes for us as well as the men, two guns, a baseball bat and a box of canned food later, and we were finished.

With a grimace, I shut the tailgate and sighed. With only a few hours of sunlight left, this was all we'd be able to get today.

"Not a bad haul. Could be better," Annabelle said.

I nodded but only agreed that it could have been better. It wasn't enough food.

I'd stepped around the truck, ready to head back to the guys when I heard the rumble.

"Do you hear that?" Annabelle asked at the same time. "Sounds like an engine. A big one."

We were parked at the first house in the neighborhood, just a few feet from the main road. The entrance had one of those brick signs with the name of the subdivision on it, along with several tall trees that probably were planted to give the residents a feeling of privacy.

Annabelle and I looked at each other, acknowledging that both of our curiosity had been stroked. Running toward the sign, we crouched behind the bricks and waited. But as the loud grinding noise came closer, it became obvious that it wasn't coming from just one engine.

Peeking around the bricks, we watched as three semi-trucks barreled towards us. The first one had massive trailers attached to the back. But it was the next truck that had Annabelle gasping next to me. "Oh, my god."

Oh, my god was right. The cage-like bed on the second semi was one used for transporting livestock. Except, this one was filled with flesh-eaters.

2

MINUTES LATER, THE TRUCKS WERE LONG GONE, BUT neither Anabelle or I had moved from our hiding spot, still processing what we'd just witnessed.

"That was fucked up," Annabelle gasped.

I couldn't have agreed more. *"Come on,"* I signed. *"We need to tell the guys about this."*

But as we got close to the truck, motion out of the corner of my eye stopped me. I had my knife out and in front of me in a defensive position before the boy could take another step closer.

Anabelle swung around at my move and took a step back to stand next to me, but surprisingly, the boy didn't even flinch. No older than twelve or thirteen, he stood several feet away, his dark eyes steady and watchful as they bounced between Annabelle and me. Though skinny, he didn't look malnourished. And his clothes had fewer holes than mine. Wherever he came from, he'd been well taken care of. The thought eased my mind.

After several tense seconds passed with no one saying a word, my friend finally broke the silence. "Geez, kid.

Don't you know sneaking up on people is rude? You could have given us girls a heart attack. Then what would you have done, hmm?"

The boy's face broke out into a grin, and the mood immediately lightened.

"You're funny," he said in a surprisingly deep voice.

Annabelle shrugged. "I try. I'm Annabelle, what's your name?" she asked.

"Fredrick."

"Nice to meet ya. So whatcha doing out here, Fredrick?"

The boy watched me put away my knife as he spoke. "I saw the trucks coming and tried to warn you, but I didn't make it in time. I'm glad you hid."

"Warn us about what?" Annabelle asked.

"The mad scientists."

My eyes widened as they connected with Annabelle's. Mad scientists? The CDC? A coincidence?

"I have to go now," he said, about to turn away.

"Wait," Annabelle called, lifting a hand. "What mad scientists?"

The look he gave us over his small shoulder was so sad, I swallowed with no small amount of fear of what he was about to say.

"Dad says they used to be good scientists, but now we have to hide from them."

"Can you tell us where they are?" When he shook his head no, she tried again. "They have a friend of ours."

"Then he's already dead, or worse," a man said as he stepped out from behind the house. He came to stand next to the boy, putting his hand on Fredrick's shoulder.

My hands balled into fists at my sides at the ready, the

presence of the boy the only reason I hadn't gone for my knife again.

"Sorry," he said to me, his eyes dropping from my face to my clenched fist and back. He raised his hands, palms out. "I wish you no harm. I only mean to warn you. My name is Tyrone, and this is my son, Fredrick. Though I guess he's already told you that." He looked down at his son and raised an eyebrow. "We're going to have to have another discussion about talking to strangers."

"I'm Annabelle, and this is my friend, Jane," Annabelle said.

Releasing my fists, I signed, *"Hello."* At Frederick's widening eyes, I gave him a friendly smile.

"I'm sorry." Tyrone's brows puckered as he looked at Annabelle. "I don't know sign language."

"She just said hello," she told him. "But don't worry, she can hear you. Jane's mute, not deaf."

He nodded his head. "Word of advice then," he said to both of us, "don't go searching for these people. They're worse monsters than the flesh-eaters."

"Please," Annabelle spoke softly, though her clenched jaw said she was getting as frustrated as me. "We need to find our friend."

The man sighed but nodded. "I've warned you, that's all I can do." He pointed to where the trucks had disappeared. "Three miles north of here. I'll give you directions, but it won't be easy. I located the hidden cave a few months back and never could find a way in."

His haunted gaze looked down at the boy. "I wish you better luck than me. We've all lost too much as it is."

3

AFTER WE LEFT THE SUBDIVISION, I COULDN'T GET Tyrone and Fredrick out of my head. The look in Tyrone's eyes when he'd spoken about the hidden cave and the mad scientists within made me suspect he'd been searching for someone. Had they taken someone he loved? Maybe Fredrick's mom? The thought made my blood boil, the rage causing my need to find the facility even stronger.

I'd wanted to follow those trucks and Tyrone's directions right then, but Annabelle convinced me we needed to tell the guys first. And of course, they wanted to wait until morning to start searching.

Kaden hadn't been happy about us speaking to Tyrone, reminding me of when Tyrone had scolded Fredrick for talking to strangers. I'd responded to Kaden with a well-deserved finger gesture and a comment about him not being my daddy.

Suffice it to say, Kaden wasn't speaking to me at the moment. Which made things a bit awkward on the drive.

Anabelle had abandoned me to ride with Aidan. I'd get her back later.

"There," Kaden said with a nod for me to follow his line of sight. He turned onto an overgrown dirt road and slowly drove forward. Tall pines lined the road, the forest dense on either side. It reminded me a little of the entrance to our farm, making me suddenly homesick.

Ten minutes later, the road abruptly ended. Kaden parked the truck and we hopped out, gesturing for Aidan and Anabelle to do the same.

"What's going on?" Aidan asked.

Kaden gestured to the small trail leading deeper into the woods. "Looks like we have to go on foot."

After grabbing our packs, we set off for what I expected to be a long hike. But our trek ended just as quick as it began.

"That wasn't as hard as I thought it would be," Anabelle spoke aloud my thoughts as we all ducked behind some brush.

It didn't look like anything special. Hidden by the trees on an incline about thirty feet away, we surveyed the dense forest surrounding us. Just below, the mouth of the cave yawned from the hillside. Obscured by large boulders and green vegetation, no one would have noticed the entrance if they weren't looking for it.

I wiped the accumulating moisture on my forehead away with the back of my hand and looked up at the darkening sky. Right now, it was only misting. Our elevation was high enough that the humidity had lowered, but the air had also chilled, causing my damp skin to prickle.

The only jacket I'd packed was made of lightweight cotton and would probably be soaked through by the end of the day, but it would do. If I hadn't been so distracted arguing with Kaden, I would have grabbed a poncho. Kaden had a way of stripping away all of my good sense. So had Mason, come to think of it.

"We're going to get a closer look at the entrance," Kaden said to me. "And maybe see if we can find another entry point. Those trucks have to be coming and going from somewhere."

"I can help," I signed.

Our eyes locked and held. His gaze darkened and narrowed before he finally sighed. "I could really use you and Anabelle to keep watch. Use the two-way radio if you see anyone."

I pressed my lips together, not happy to just sit and wait, but I agreed with a nod.

"Thank you," he said, his expression so relieved my eyes widened. Then in a surprising move, he gripped the back of my head and pressed a hard kiss to my open lips. His tongue flicked, coaxing me to respond. I melted, giving us both what we wanted.

The kiss was short but had been passionate enough to make my toes curl.

"I'll be back soon," he growled, his gaze burning me up as he backed away.

I shook off the effects of his dark promise, but it was no good. No matter how angry I became, I could never get enough of Kaden. Instead, I chose to ignore it for now.

Annabelle and I took watched quietly from our perch, binoculars glued to our faces. From our vantage point, nothing could be seen inside the cave but darkness. But somewhere, deep inside the nothingness, was our way in. I tried searching for Kaden, but he was good at not being seen. If Aidan's voice hadn't crackled through the two-way, I would have thought they'd vanished into thin air.

"We spotted security cameras," he said.

"Should we change our location?" Annabelle asked.

"No. You're safe."

"Be careful," she told him, lowering the two-way before speaking to me. "Maybe we should rush in. Surprise the hell out of 'em, you know? We have the C4 Kaden found. We could blow the doors wide open."

Kaden had run across an abandoned convoy while on a supply run. Most of the weapons had been picked through, but somehow a block of C4 had been missed. The only thing stopping us from storming the place was the security cameras we'd spotted.

"They'd see us coming," I reminded Annabelle.

"I know," she said. "But maybe we'd get in before they could react." Though, her voice said she wasn't confident with that plan.

Annabelle sighed next to me, and I agreed. Both of us knew what it took to survive. How to wait patiently for the right time to either strike or run. But this was different. None of us wanted to think about what they were doing to Mason while we strategized. Our strategy so far, however, comprised of nothing more than scouting the area and looking for the best entry point.

Truthfully, Annabelle wasn't the only impatient one. Every second of waiting, searching, and planning only produced more unease. I was good at sneaking around, but Kaden was right. There had to be a back entrance for those trucks. Even an emergency exit, an air vent, or something.

Annabelle dropped her arms onto her bent knees and

turned to me. She had a glint in her eye that made me wary. "So... what's up with you and Kaden?" she asked.

The muscles in my neck stiffened a half a second before I could catch myself.

"Ah-ha," she exclaimed with a whisper. "I knew there was something going on. The tension between the two of you is so thick, even Poco has been keeping his distance. You haven't forgiven him, have you? Even though he's apologized a million times."

Turning away from her critical gaze, I looked through the binoculars, seeing nothing but Kaden's sad expression when I'd pulled away from him after we'd had sex. It reminded me of Poco's earnest gaze when we left him behind to search for the facility. We'd all agreed it was too dangerous until we knew what we were dealing with. Did Kaden think I was going to leave him behind? *No, that was his specialty.* The bitter thought was unfair, and I shoved it away.

Annabelle was watching me expectantly, but I didn't know what to say. Hell, I didn't understand my own feelings. How was I supposed to explain it to someone else?

Things between Kaden and I were... tense, as Annabelle had clearly observed. Stilted, even. Forgiving him should have been easy enough. I'd thought I had. But slowly, those feelings of abandonment resurfaced along with the acknowledgment that he could leave again. Most likely would, actually. Maybe not even on his own terms. The amount of death I'd seen in the last few years taught me how fleeting our time on this earth was.

No, I hadn't quite let go of my anger and resentment. I needed to either forgive and forget or move on. But for the time being, I would enjoy what was left of us, the physical parts of our relationship. The attraction, the pull between us… that, at least, hadn't changed.

"You know, what they did was shitty," Anabelle said, surprising me enough that I whipped my head around. She gave me a half smile. "I'm on your side, Jane. They weren't wrong for leaving the way they did, or for asking you to leave them. They were just trying to protect you. But they were wrong for staying away so long. I think you should talk to them. Well, you should talk to Kaden. Then when we get Mason back, the three of you can discuss it. Eventually, you'll get through it. They're good guys, and I think they can make you happy."

After her little speech, she sat quiet, letting her words steep. I especially admired her optimism.

She was right, though. As simple as that, I knew she was. But saying and doing were two different things.

"Hey, you want to change position?" she asked.

As we climbed the cliff edge, we were careful to keep as much brush between us and the possible cameras. Then we continued moving east for about a quarter of a mile to the opposite side of the cave entrance.

While we walked, I had an opportunity to give as good as I'd gotten. It was my turn to stick my nose in my friend's business.

"How are things with you and Aidan?" I asked.

"Great," she said, not at all annoyed that I'd asked.

"It took a little while for him to come around, but in the end, he couldn't resist my expert seduction skills." She wiggled her eyebrows while licking her lips awkwardly. It came off looking ridiculous, and I couldn't help but smile.

"Hey, it worked!" Anabelle exclaimed softly, bumping my shoulder with hers. "Especially once I convinced him I wasn't jailbait."

I raised an eyebrow. Annabelle was young, but not that young.

By the time we found a spot that afforded a decent view, the rain had turned from misting to a steady drizzle. Thankfully, Annabelle had been smart enough to bring the right supplies.

As she unrolled the dark green tarp, I scanned the wide expanse of trees and undergrowth above and beyond the cave entrance. My mind immediately went to Mason. He was down there, below the forest, where they were doing experiments and who knew what else. The more I thought about it, the crazier it made me. He was immune to whatever turned humans into flesh-eaters. And while the thought comforted me some, he had volunteered to be a guinea pig. It had been courageous, and something I couldn't fault him for. But I didn't like the thought of him all alone in there. Suffering… maybe dying. What would they do to him in the name of science? What wouldn't they do?

Once the tarp was unrolled, we secured it using rope, tying the four ends to the trunks of two nearby trees. Then we huddled underneath.

"Aidan thought you were underage?" I asked, once settled.

"Not really," she shrugged. "More like, he just thought I was too young for him. Which is ridiculous, of course. And I told him so. Especially given that he's only six years older than me. We're still working out the kinks," she grinned, wiggling her eyebrows once again.

I shook my head at her and did a scan of the area, seeing nothing but green, green, and more green with a tint of gray and brown from the boulders. All muted from the rain and gray sky above. Spring in the Appalachian Mountains could be one of the most beautiful sights.

Unless you have to stare at the same trees and plants for hours on end.

Just before lowering the binoculars, I caught movement and stilled. At first, I almost dismissed the waving of tree limbs. It could have been anything, from the rain or the wind to a bird or a squirrel. This area was teaming with wildlife. Even black bears weren't uncommon. But it wasn't a bear that staggered through the underbrush.

Covered in brown filth, the only spot of color was the red gaping wound where an arm used to be. He stumbled and tripped, walking aimlessly through the trees, too far away to hear, see, or smell us. It was clear he wasn't a threat.

I would have pointed out the flesh-eater to Annabelle so we could keep an eye on it in case it came any closer, but suddenly it wasn't alone. There'd been only a flesh-eater, wobbling on his feet, then out of nowhere, there'd been another person. A live person, in military fatigues.

"Want something to eat?" Annabelle asked, startling me.

"I have some jerky and a jar of applesauce," she said, digging through her bag. "So glad we thought to bring some of the canned stuff from the farmhouse before we left. We're getting down to the last of it, though... Where the hell are they? Damn jars fell to the bottom somewhere. Hope they didn't break."

The flesh-eater reached for the guy, it's dead fingers clawing air as it closed in. But the guy was prepared. He slipped a noose end of a catcher's pole around the flesh-eater's neck. My sudden intake of air caused Annabelle to laugh, thinking it was for the wrong reasons.

The guy gave the catcher poll a jerk, causing the flesh-eater to stumble forward, then he turned and… He was gone. I frantically searched the area. The man had disappeared as quickly as he'd appeared. Where had he gone? A secret entrance maybe?

"Jane… Jane?"

I turned toward Annabelle's voice. She gave me a concerned look while holding out a jar of applesauce. "Did you see something?" she asked, picking up her binoculars. Seeing nothing, she turned questioning eyes my way. Reluctantly, I signed, *"Call Aidan."* Then I explained while she translated what I'd seen to the guys.

"Damn. We could have followed him." Kaden's tone held no accusation, but I felt like he was asking without asking why I hadn't said something sooner.

"It happened fast," I defended myself out of guilt.

Anabelle repeated what I signed, then asked, "Want us to go check it out?"

"No," Aidan replied. "We'll take a look and meet you at the cars in two hours."

"Will do."

With a sigh, Anabelle passed me a bottle of water and my portion of the jerky. As we ate in silence, my mind turned. Something didn't feel right. I wanted to search the area, badly. And I wanted to do it alone. I just had to figure out a way.

4

INSECTS SCATTERED IN THE BEAM OF MY FLASHLIGHT AS I swept it over the forest floor, searching the ground for signs of a disturbance or footprints. The guy has disappeared with the flesh-eater so quickly there was only one explanation. There had to be a hidden access tunnel. But so far, at least an hour had passed since I'd started the search, and I worried the rain had washed away any clue that what I'd seen was even real. Night had fallen and Kaden was sure to have begun searching for me by now. But I was determined to find this secret entrance.

Getting away from the group unnoticed hadn't been as hard as I'd thought it would be. After we'd returned the house, I begged off from going with Kaden to fill up the trucks with gas, claiming exhaustion. At the thought of him going alone, worry had tightened into a knot in my stomach. But I hadn't argued that he should take Aidan or Annabelle along. I made a mental note to point it out to him later that trust between us would go a long way.

Then again, when he found out what I'd done, he was

going to be pissed. It probably wouldn't be the best time to start a conversation about trust.

Once Kaden had left in search of supplies, I'd waited for Annabelle and Aidan to close themselves off in their bedroom, gave a whining Poco a quick scratch behind his ears, then snuck out the door.

No longer raining, the night air had grown warm and thick, causing my skin to dampen with sweat beneath my light jacket. The mountains were a strange mix of quiet and loud. The chirp of hundreds of crickets and katydids were interrupted sporadically by the peaceful hoot of an owl or call of other nocturnal birds. If I sat still long enough, the unobtrusive noise could coax me to sleep in mere seconds.

Lightening flashed in the distance and at the count of ten, the boom shook the earth beneath my feet. It wouldn't be much longer before the storm arrived, and I'd be forced to call it a night.

Squatting next to a patch of Virginia Bluebells, my fingers sifted through the dead leaves and soil beneath. Finding nothing more, I stood up straight to stretch my back before walking a few steps further. I was working in rows, walking from one tree I'd mentally marked to another before moving a few feet to sweep another line.

The beam of the flashlight shown on a broken branch, and I stepped gingerly in that direction, searching the ground. Bending down, I brushed a few dead leaves aside and smiled at the booted footprint that was almost twice as big as mine. About three feet away was another. Now all I needed to do was follow.

As I prepared to stand, the leaves undulated next to my boot. I froze for half a second before the light brown head of a snake made an appearance. Its tongue flickered toward my left foot, and I scrambled back through the wet ferns, falling onto my ass. I'd managed to put ten feet between me and the snake in two seconds flat.

Heart racing, I swept the flashlight beam in a frantic circle around me, not finding any sign of the copperhead. Lightening cracked above causing me to jump. I huffed, silently laughing at myself. Snakes didn't usually scare me unless they were the poisonous kind. That had been a close call.

Another bolt of lightning lit the night, and I scrambled to my knees. Wet leaves slid over my cheeks as I crawled across the forest floor. A flash of metal caught my eye and I pushed the foliage away, revealing a hidden steel door with two handgrips. I gave one an experimental tug, surprised when the door lifted. I'd been half expecting it to be locked.

My flashlight revealed a set of stairs centered in the middle of a steel pipe leading down into nothingness. Staring deep into the dark hole, I second-guessed myself. Now that I'd found it, I could go back, tell the others. It's what I should have done if I were smart. Or I could take a peek, find out if the tunnel even takes us to the facility. Then once I knew for sure, I'd go back for Kaden, Annabelle, and Aidan. It could save us time. And an added bonus was that no one but me would be put in danger.

A bolt of lightning struck the ground nearby, the crack reverberating throughout the forest. Seconds later, rain fell from the sky in sheets, soaking me instantly. Quickly, I stepped into the pipe and walked down the stairs until I could pull the door shut. The wind picked up, blowing in the perfect direction to aid my efforts. As loud as the clap of thunder outside, the door slammed above me before giving an ominous click and plunging me into darkness.

I shoved at the door with the palm of my hand, but it wouldn't budge. The beam of my flashlight landed on the CDC logo, which was right next to the only access to unlock the door, a keycard reader.

What was that about being smart? Well, I never claimed to be a genius.

5

WITH NOWHERE ELSE TO GO BUT DOWN, I STEADIED MY flashlight and watched my steps carefully. As I descended, the sound of the storm outside gradually disappeared, replaced by the slow drip, drip of water echoing throughout the pipe. At the bottom, the pipe ended where cave walls began, along with a two-foot-wide concrete walkway. Dim yellow lights swung from wooden beams that were used to support the low hanging ceilings. The air was musty and dank and reminded me of the time my parents and I toured the Hoover Dam. I remembered being afraid to walk through the dimly-lit tunnel, even with the large group we'd been with. The thought of being underground, buried alive, was a real fear. Something I hadn't thought about until just this moment.

After taking a deep breath, I bottled the fear, reminding myself that the only way out was to go forward. I slid the flashlight into my back pocket for now and kept going.

Not wanting to be dragged down, I'd brought nothing with me but the flashlight and my weapons, which were hidden on my person as usual. I had one knife strapped to my right ankle and another on my hip. I'd thought about bringing a gun or two, but if I needed more than my knives to get out of here, then I probably wasn't leaving anyhow.

A sudden prickle of foreboding caused the back of my neck to tingle, but I shook off my sudden unease. Even if I were caught sneaking in, what would they do? Kick me out? Naahir had threatened me, but I had a feeling that here, under the thumb of the CDC and the government, he didn't have as much power. Most of his talk was just that, talk. A way to get Mason to do his bidding. They needed Mason because he was immune to flesh-eater bites. I, on the other hand, had nothing they wanted.

It felt like the tunnel went on forever before it eventually widened to almost the size of a two-lane highway. I could see the opening of a second passageway, but a deep rumbling sound slowed my steps. With my back to the cave wall, I peeked around the corner, surprised to see a semi-truck with its engine running. The trailer was backed up to a two-door loading dock. Though there were no people in the tunnels that I could see, I could hear men from the other side of the station calling out orders. As they opened the trailer, the screech of metal echoed off the walls and I winced, then froze in horror when the familiar sound of chattering teeth was followed by the stench of rotting flesh.

I saw no flesh-eaters, but could hear and smell them clearly, as if they stood right next to me. And it wasn't the sound or scent of a few. There had to be hundreds of them in there. Just like the truck Annabelle and I had seen the day before.

The shock over what I was witnessing had me rooted

to the spot, and unfortunately heedless of the footsteps approaching quietly behind me.

"I always knew you were a troublemaker. Be a dear and turn around slowly with your hands where I can see them. You're much too good with those knives of yours."

Closing my eyes, I cursed at myself before doing what he told me. Hands in the air, I turned to see the handsome, smiling face of the one man I'd hoped not to run into. Next to him were three soldiers, each pointing their rifles in my direction. I was totally screwed.

"Good of you to join us," Naahir said as he walked boldly up to me. I itched to grab the knife at my hip and take care of this scumbag once and for all, but the position of his body didn't go unnoticed. All three soldiers had a clear shot if I were to make a move.

Stopping boot to boot, his dark gaze penetrated mine, and I lifted my chin. His grin only widened. "Yes," he whispered. "You are a troublemaker, indeed."

Then he flipped me around so suddenly I almost lost my balance. My palms slapped the wall seconds before my face would have.

"You might be surprised to know that I'm glad you came to visit, Jane," Naahir said as he briskly patted me down. He pulled the knife from of its sheath at my hip and dropped it to the floor.

"It's true," he continued as if I'd argued. "With Mason helping us, we've made a lot of progress. But we still have so much work to do." His hands found the second blade and he tsked.

Once he removed my last weapon, he stood and pressed close. I held my breath as his breath blew across my ear. "Let me show you what we've accomplished."

A sharp sting at the base of my neck spread heat

across my skin like a lick of flames and caused my jaw to clench in pain. As my fighting instincts took over, Naahir held me tightly against him until my body slackened, and darkness crowded my vision.

"Goodnight, Jane."

6

THE POUNDING IN MY SKULL AND THE SUDDEN SHARP ODOR of disinfectant woke me. My head felt fuzzy, like someone had stuffed it full of cotton. Scrunching up my nose, I peeled my eyes open and blinked to make sure what I was seeing was real. A tile floor? It took a moment, but I soon realized I was lying on my stomach on a bed that had an opening for my face. Cool air passed over my naked back and I sucked in a sharp breath. But when I tried to get up, I couldn't move. As my heartbeat quickened, a series of beeps sounded, like an alarm. Then a set of familiar eyes appeared in front of me from below.

"Hello, Jane." Though her voice was muffled from a surgical mask, I recognized it immediately and my eyes widened. She was the doctor I'd met at Naahir's compound. Dr. Young.

"I see that you recognize me," Dr. Young said, her eyes smiling. "Dr. Chadwick and I are excited to work with you. When we find a cure, your sacrifice to humanity will be greatly appreciated."

My face must have registered confusion, but she disappeared from view without further explanation.

"And Jane," she said from above, her voice so icy a shiver crept down my spine, "I'm sorry about the lack of anesthesia."

Before I could grasp her meaning, there was a sudden pressure in my lower back. I tried to pull away, but I could do nothing but watch helplessly as my tears splashed onto the tile below. As the force in my back morphed from uncomfortable into something sharper, I forgot to breathe. Then the pain exploded, and all I could do was scream in silence.

7

WITH A POWERFUL JOLT, I OPENED MY EYES AND WINCED AT the blinding light above. My immediate reflex was to cover my face, but my arm didn't heed my body's simple command. A quick glance showed me the thick leather straps wrapped around my wrists were the culprits, and my legs were equally immobile. My tugging was fruitless and as I gained lucidity, the less I fought the restraints. I remembered now. There was no use struggling. This time, I couldn't fight my way out.

Bright white surrounded me; the walls, ceiling, and floors were closing in on me. The only refuge, the fourth wall directly across from the bed, was made of crystal clear glass. But my gaze found nothing more to see. Beyond the glass door only held more of the same white emptiness.

My chest rose and fell rapidly as I let my head fall back to the bed with a thump. I was weak. I could feel the fragility in my bones and unused muscles. I hadn't walked on my own in God knew how long. I'd stopped measuring time after the first few days. Once the tests and injections had begun, I'd spent a lot of time sleeping. Whatever they'd been injecting into me had caused me to be all but useless. Even the small amount of strength it had taken to pull on my restraints had been too much. This was the first time in a while that I could actually think properly and it was frightening. A part of me begged for sleep once more, where I could exist in my memories. Even reliving my mistakes was better than this reality.

The familiar swoosh of the sliding glass door opening froze my racing heart. The sound had every muscle in my body tense, but it was the person who walked into the room that had my stomach clenching in fear.

He'd never introduced himself personally, but his nametag had revealed him to be Dr. Thomas H. Chadwick Jr. I'd been surprised. I would have expected such an evil man to have a more unique name.

With a quick glance, Dr. Chadwick checked to make sure my restraints had held strong, then his attention went back to the tablet in his hands. His white coat was as clean and bright as the room, making his short, dark hair stand out in contrast. Like the other times I'd seen him, the bottom half of his face was covered with a mask. He'd never spoken or looked directly at me. And when he would touch me, it was only to inflict pain with his large, cold hands.

My gaze fastened to those hands as he tapped the screen of his tablet. He stood close to the bed, and though I could see the screen, the mixture of numbers, words, and graphs were unfamiliar. I blinked, surprised at how clear my vision and mind were, and I realized the nurse hadn't come in with the usual injection.

As fuzzy as my memory was, I had recognized the routine. A nurse would give me a shot of some sort of muscle relaxant, usually a few minutes before the doctor arrived. My hands clenched into fists at my sides. My muscles were definitely not relaxed. Something was different.

"Test subject H5562, round two of testing complete," Dr. Chadwick said, in a low, toneless voice, completely devoid of emotion. I'd learned early on that he wasn't speaking to me, but into a recording app on his tablet.

I'd also learned that listening to him recite every tortuous test they'd put me through only caused me anxiety. Tuning him out, I took a deep breath. The scent of bleach burned my nose, but it was a good distraction. Still, the need to run hammered at me along with the rapid beat of my pulse.

I closed my eyes in defeat. There was no use panicking over something I couldn't control. There would be no escape. At least not physically. If only I could go back in time. My biggest mistake had been in underestimating Naahir. Or maybe it had been coming to the facility alone. I'd bet my life on that one.

And speaking of Naahir, I hadn't seen him since, that I could remember. His absence filled me with both relief and uneasiness.

"Vitals are normal. Subject H5562 is ready for phase three. Dr. Young, bring in subject Z11983."

The words brought me out of my head, but it was the sound of my nightmares coming through the glass sliding door that sent ice water flowing through my veins.

Eyes impossibly wide, my gaze focused on the chattering teeth of the flesh-eater stumbling into the room. Agitated, the click-clacking of the flesh-eater's teeth grew louder at the sight of me. It did its best to lunge forward, but Dr. Young held tight to a catcher pole as she maneuvered the flesh-eater further into the room.

I'd been frozen when they'd entered, but when they didn't stop and continued to get closer to the bed, I panicked. My wrists and ankles burned with the strength of my struggles, but the thick leather restraints didn't budge.

I jerked, surprised when the doctor leaned over my torso to unbuckle the strap around my right wrist. Then he stepped back, his cold eyes on Dr. Young as she brought the flesh-eater closer. Realizing he wasn't going to help me, I immediately pulled my arm free and reached for the strap at my opposite wrist, doing my best to hurry. My best wasn't good enough.

On instinct, I threw my free arm into the air to protect my neck when the flesh-eater lunged. Its bony fingers gripped me with so much force, I couldn't pull away. Then agony shot through my entire body as its teeth sunk into the flesh of my forearm. Blood spurted from the wound, splattering across my face and torso. A mixture of blood, sweat, and tears, ran into my eyes, and my vision blurred. The pain was so intense I begged for darkness, but it was long in coming.

It ended just as suddenly as it had begun. From behind the flesh-eater, now gnawing on my arm like a dog with a bone, Dr. Young pressed something metallic against its head and pulled the trigger. It made a little popping sound and the flesh-eater fell to the floor.

In my state of complete exhaustion and torment, I'd missed the body being cleaned away until I opened my eyes and it was gone. Nor had I noticed Dr. Chadwick moving to the other side of the bed. Searing pain made my vision go gray as he lifted my ravaged arm. I writhed while he twisted it one way, then the other as he examined the wound.

"The bite is more than sufficient," he spoke aloud in that detached voice of his, and I added torture to my list of all the ways I was going to kill him. Then I made the mistake of looking at my throbbing limb. A chunk of flesh had been torn off, and the white of bone peeked through the bright red mess that used to be my forearm. And that was my limit. My eyes rolled to the back of my head and everything went dark.

"Phase three complete."

When I eventually came to, the first thing I noticed was the lack of pain in my arm. Though only a dull throb remained, not much time could have passed if the still drying blood on my gown was any indication. The second thing I detected was that the restraint was still missing from my wrist. And I wasn't alone.

Dr. Young wheeled a small table over to the bed and placed a metal tray on top. I watched her under half-closed eyelids, doing my best not to flinch as she cleaned the bite on my forearm. She wasn't particularly gentle. Not that it surprised me. All I was to them was a lab rat. I'd seen the truth displayed in their callous eyes as they looked at me. I was a test subject and nothing more. And if I didn't get out of here, I would die for whatever cause they felt was worthy of torture.

As she bandaged the wound, my furtive gaze landed on the ID card clipped to the chest pocket of her scrubs. There was no name or picture, only a six-digit number, and a barcode. My gaze then slipped to the metal tray and the instruments gleaming under the florescent lights. Next to the gauze was a syringe filled and uncapped, ready to be administered. Thinking about all the injections they'd given me caused my forehead to bead with sweat. But I pushed the tortuous imagery down and bided my time.

Dr. Young glanced up and noticed me watching her. "Oh good, you're awake," she said, giving my arm a squeeze. The corners of her lips lifting slightly when I winced.

"Don't worry. It won't hurt for long," she said.

Because as a flesh-eater, I'll no longer feel pain?

She swabbing the wound with something that burned like fire, and I gritted my teeth through the pain, putting all my energy into not passing out. There was still time before the symptoms began and I planned on using that time to my advantage.

Dr. Young reached for something on the tray that wasn't there. Sighing, she spun on the stool, putting her back to me as she opened a drawer. My gaze fell to the tray, noticing a filled syringe.

"Dr. Chadwick is optimistic, but I have serious doubts that his vaccine will work. It didn't last time. Though, I do believe he may have made a few tweaks since then."

She spun back around and shrugged. "Guess we'll find out." Then her brown eyes lit up. "I'm sure you're wondering about Mason. He's doing well. In fact, I work with him personally, and he's been a tremendous help. The two of us have gotten close." She leaned in as if to divulge a secret. "Very close," she whispered, her eyelids lowering shyly. "And we are—

Dr. Young broke off with a gasp and I pressed on the plunger, administering whatever had been in that syringe meant for me.

It had been an awkward angle but not impossible. I'd held it like a baseball bat and lifted my arm, jamming it into the closest place I could reach. Which happened to have been where her shoulder met her neck, thanks to her leaning over to whisper in my ear.

She jumped to her feet and stumbled back, tripping over the stool. But she righted herself and with a smirk, yanked the needle from her neck. "You think you're so smart," she said, though the words were almost too slurred to understand. "I'm not..." she shook her head. "I mean... You're not..." Her eyes rolled up until only the whites shown. Then she finally dropped to the floor.

I released the rest of my restraints and hopped from the bed. The quick motion had been a stupid mistake. The room spun, and I had to grab hold of the bed to keep from falling. After a few moments, the dizziness passed. But what I hadn't counted on was how weak my legs were. I couldn't remember the last time I'd walked, and the thought of having to run made me rethink this escape plan. Though one look at the unconscious doctor and I knew there was no going back now.

With shaking hands and wobbly knees, I removed Dr. Young's ID badge. If I'd had the strength, I would have put her on the bed. It would have given me more time if someone happened to walk by after I left.

A sudden thought had my eyes scanning every corner of the room. I'd forgotten about the cameras. Again. Though a swift glance around showed no signs of them. Not taking any chances, I staggered to the glass door and found a familiar looking key card reader. I held up Dr. Young's badge, smiling when the door slid open, and I stepped out into the empty hallway. Finally, something was going right. Now I just had to decide which way to go.

To the right was an unlabeled door. To the left, the corridor went on for several feet before veering right. Neither had a sign with bright neon arrows pointing to where I'd find Mason. If I were only looking for a way out, I would have gone with the way most likely to lead me to an exit. But I couldn't leave without Mason.

The first room I came to was identical to mine. A body lay motionless on the bed, and only from the rise and fall of his chest, did I know he was alive. I took my time looking at his face, noticing the pallor of his skin, the deep purple bruises under his eyes, and the sharpness of his cheekbones. He was so thin. I wondered how he could still be alive. My jaw clenched. The anger burning through my veins had me rolling my eyes toward the ceiling. But for maybe the hundredth time since I'd woken in this godforsaken place, I set aside the rage and focused on making it out of there alive. Revenge, I vowed, would come later, and it would be mine.

Each room I passed was identical to the next, and all of them were occupied by a single person lying still on the bed. None of them had been Mason.

Running footsteps and male voices caused me to look over my shoulder. They hadn't found me yet, but they were close. I rushed to unlock the closest door, slamming it closed behind me. The corridor I'd entered was long, and though I needed to put as much distance between me and the men as quickly as I could, my steps were shaky and slow. I cursed my weakness when I had to support myself against the wall for a moment and catch my breath.

Thump.

The sudden sound made me flinch, but it was the sight of the flesh-eater that had every muscle in my body constricting. It had nothing but muscle and bone left. And as its jaw moved up and down in the familiar way that I knew, I waited to hear the clacking of its teeth. Though, all I heard was silence thanks to the glass separating the two of us.

When it slammed its arms against the glass with another thump, I flinched once more. But it wasn't alone. And was soon joined by another, then another.

As more flesh-eaters moved up from behind him and fell onto the glass, real terror seeped into my bones. The room was filled with them. Twenty, no fifty, at least. A quick glance told me there were six rooms. Were they all filled with flesh-eaters? Or was it only this one? I shuddered at the thought of a person lying in a bed with no clue what was next to them.

Taking a shaky breath, I took a step forward. I couldn't go back. Not now. There wasn't time. Though I didn't have the energy to run, I moved as fast as possible. And soon learned that each of those six rooms held so many flesh-eaters that by the time I reached the end of the hallway, I swore I could hear them. The click-clacking of their teeth, together with the thumping on the glass, was so loud my hands shook.

The ID trembled in my grasp, taking several passes through the lock before the green light finally appeared. I swept open the door and slammed it shut, leaving me in blissful silence.

Though exhausted, I didn't stop there. I couldn't. Several turns later, I realized something looked different. There were no glass walls. When the hall came to a split, I turned left and used the badge to open yet another locked door.

"Don't worry about Jane."

My head slowly lifted as Naahir's deep voice floated

out from the open doorway on my left. Panicked, I did a quick scan of the empty hallway. This one was shorter than the others, with only two non-descript doors.

"She's here though, right?" Mason asked, and I closed my eyes in relief. "I saw her. She was in a wheelchair," he said, his voice rising. "That was three days ago. What have you done with her?"

My eyes widened at the information, and I had a sudden memory of white walls zipping by me in a haze. It had been after the procedure on my back. Afterwards, I'd been in pain and pretty out of it. And the motion had caused my stomach to roll and my muscles to clench in an effort to not puke.

Someone had called my name, and I'd tried to sit upright, but my head had rested limply on my shoulder. My limbs had been useless, either because of the drugs or from the restraints, I wasn't sure.

"We can't keep her here much longer," I remembered Naahir telling Dr. Chadwick later. *"We can't have Mr. Reed becoming… unmanageable."*

"It won't be much longer," the doctor had replied. I shivered at the memory.

"Jane?" Naahir's voice brought me back to the present. "I did nothing to her. She volunteered just like you did."

"I don't believe you," Mason said, but his voice faltered.

"Believe what you want. Jane is doing us a service. A service you offered, but are now refusing," Naahir said a little closer this time.

Frantic, I slipped into the partially open door to my right. The room was dark, and thankfully, empty. I turned to close the door, leaving only a small sliver to look through.

"I'd be more than happy to help if you'd take me to Jane. I've told them this," Mason said.

"I don't have the authority here to do your bidding," Naahir said smoothly.

"And I don't care if it were the janitor or the president of the United States who took me to her. But until someone does, I'm not doing shit for you or anyone else here."

I raised my brows at the threatening tone in Mason's voice and held my breath for Naahir's answer.

There was a long pause, but eventually, he replied. "I wouldn't make promises you can't keep. Willing or not, you will be assisting us."

The door made a light click, and I rushed to close it just as footsteps drew closer. Pressing my forehead to the door, I listened carefully as Naahir passed where I hid, blowing out a relieved breath when I heard the faint sound of the corridor door opening and closing. But my relief was short lived when I realized he was headed the same way I'd just come. I took several turns to get here, but it still wouldn't surprise me if he were to head straight to my room after his conversation with Mason.

My legs were shaking, I was so tired, but I had to push through. Knowing there was little time before someone discovered me missing, I swung open the door, ready to rush to Mason's side, only to stumble back when a body filled up the doorway halting my exit.

"What are you doing here, Jane?"

I blinked up at Mason, surprised, but delighted to see him. My hands lifted, ready to sign the plans for our escape. Instead, a wave a fatigue hit me hard and I swayed.

"Whoa!"

I had one blissful moment in Mason's arms before I passed out cold.

9

"WHAT THE HELL DID YOU DO TO HER?" MASON'S SHOUT pulled me out of unconsciousness, and at first, I was confused. People were talking, but my head was so full of cotton, I struggled to hear what they were saying, though it became increasingly obvious. The subject of their conversation was me.

"She's burning up with fever," Mason said. "And look at her! I'm done negotiating. I'm taking her, and we're getting out of here."

Someone whispered a reply I couldn't hear.

"Fuck the human race!" Mason shouted suddenly, causing me to jump.

I stilled immediately, hoping no one noticed the involuntary movement. I couldn't let on that I was awake. More than one person was in the room with us, and I needed Mason alone. I had to believe he wouldn't let them take me.

"You have no more room to negotiate." The sound of Naahir's voice almost sent me into a panic, and I had to force myself not to react.

There was a shuffling noise, then a new voice spoke. This one female. "Mason, wait," she said. "Let me talk to him."

Mason snorted. "Sure, give it a shot."

"Leave her with us, Naahir, or *I* will no longer cooperate," the woman threatened.

After a heavy pause, Naahir sighed. "Dahlia," he said in a chastising tone. "Fine. But do be warned, Mason. When she wakes up, Dr. Young will be quite upset with your Jane."

At the mention of Dr. Young, memories of being a lab rat rushed to the forefront of my mind, and I swallowed down the bile that threatened to expose me.

I'd either lost myself in the memories or I fell asleep, because the next thing I remembered, the room had become silent. A sudden pressure on my hand startled me, and I sat up too quickly. My head spun, but the need to flee pounded at me from within. I had to get up. I had to run. Take Mason and go.

Sucking in a breath, I tried again, but my body fought me.

"Hey, careful. No, lay back down. It's just me." Mason was there, pushing gently on my shoulder as he tried and failed to coerce me to relax.

I shook him off and swung my feet over the edge of the bed. *"We have to go,"* I signed.

"Go where? Wait, Jane…" Kneeling in front of me, he cupped my face in his hands, stilling my movements when I would have pulled away. Then my eyes met his, and my shoulders slumped with the reality that I'd finally found him.

His gaze ran over my face as though committing each feature to memory. I did the same. Mason didn't look half as bad as what I'd been afraid of finding. His face was a little thinner and shadows rested beneath his eyes, but he didn't look sick and had no bruises that I could see. He wore a pair of sweatpants and a t-shirt, looking much more comfortable than I was in my thin hospital gown.

One of his thumbs caressed my cheek softly as he did a scan of my body as well. His soft touch not faltering, even as his face was as hard as a rock.

"You were unconscious for about half an hour. It was the longest minutes of my life." His gaze landed on my bandaged arm. "You have blood all over your gown. What did they do to you?"

He wanted answers, and I wanted to leave. Our time was short, but being so close to Mason after weeks without him, and even longer before then, had me tied in knots. Now that he was in front of me, touching me, I had to touch him too. I ran the tips of my fingers over the collar of his shirt then onto the skin of his neck, my touch so soft, he must have barely felt it. But as I skimmed his jaw, his gaze grew soft and his lids lowered.

As we both leaned toward one another, I licked my dry lips, already remembering the taste of him on my tongue when a door opened behind me.

"Is she alright?"

I recognized the light female voice from earlier. She'd helped me. Still, every muscle in my body tensed as Mason pulled away. He cleared his throat as he stood, and I felt the loss of his attention physically.

Following his gaze, my eyes narrowed before they even rested on the woman who'd interrupted us. She stood with her arms crossed over her chest, her expression wary. Her dark eyes skittered away from me and landed on Mason, instantly lighting up. My own stare turned icy.

"She's—" Mason began, but stopped when the woman began coughing. She bent at the waist with a dry hacking cough that sounded painful to my ears.

"Dahlia!" Mason rushed to the woman's side, rubbing circles on her back as she took a few deep breaths before settling.

"I'm okay," she croaked, obviously not okay. Her golden skin had turned pasty, and her eyes were hollowed. Her clothes, which were identical to Mason's, hung loosely. Had she been subjected to the same treatments as I had?

I slid off the bed. Slowly this time. I didn't know who this chick was, but there was no time for introductions. I had to go.

Seeing Mason's attention was still on the sickly woman, I struck the bed with the palm of my hand until he afforded me a glance.

"We have to go. Now," I signed. *"Before they come back."*

Understanding dawned, and his expression hardened. "Fuck," he said with feeling. "I knew Naahir was lying. Look at you! I told him there was no way you volunteered for this." Striding back to me, he grabbed the top of my arms, his grip loosening when I sucked in a painful breath. He rubbed my sore arms in apology, and his face softened as he spoke. "I won't let them take you, Jane."

I wanted to believe him. I did. But everything in me was telling me to run.

"I can see you're about to argue, but listen to me for a minute. Sit down before you fall down."

My legs gave way, and I sat heavily on the bed, my head bowed as I fought to find my balance. Several seconds passed while I took deep breaths to calm the fuck down, reminding myself that I trusted Mason. He wouldn't purposely put me in harm's way.

When he saw that I wasn't going to flee yet, Mason sat on the bed next to me. "You heard our conversation earlier?"

I nodded. *"Some."*

"They already know you're here. I won't lie to you. They wanted to take you to another room, but I threatened them. They want my blood and my marrow and anything and everything else they can get out of me. But in order to get my cooperation, the deal was they had to leave you here with me."

His hand wrapped around mine where it was twisting the sheet into knots. Rubbing my knuckles until I relaxed, he threaded our fingers together as if he wanted to lock us together in some way. I understood.

The woman slowly made her way to a chair in the corner and sat down. As I watched her, she watched me with a cautious expression.

"We really have Dahlia to thank." Mason's words had me raising an eyebrow, though the woman never acknowledged his praise.

"Without her here, they would have taken what they wanted without my consent. She's kept them in check so far."

"Not enough, obviously," she finally spoke, her gaze still on me. "Was Mason correct? Were you an unwilling patient?"

Pressing my lips together, I nodded my head slowly. Pulling my hand out of Mason's hold, I turned to him. *"Who is she?"* I asked.

"How very rude of me," the woman said, surprising me. "My name is Dr. Dahlia Khoury. I am the director of the Center for Disease Control and Prevention. At least, I was. Dr. Chadwick has taken over most of my duties while I recover."

At the mention of Dr. Chadwick's name, I cringed, earning me a questioning look. However, she didn't ask about my reaction to her colleague.

"I know a small amount of ASL," she said. "So please, go ahead. Ask me anything."

I nodded, a little disappointed Mason and I wouldn't be able to communicate in secret around her. *"You're sick."*

"I was bitten," she said, her gaze falling on my bandage. When she looked up, I kept my face carefully blank but had a feeling I hadn't fooled her. Her eyes were knowing and surprisingly empathetic.

"I'd been very close to creating a cure," she continued. "After I was bitten, my associates finished the job. I was their first successful test. However, it wasn't as effective as we'd hoped. The virus has returned. We think with Mason's help we can find a more permanent solution."

"And it's your cooperation they want most, not Mason's. Why?" I asked. It didn't make sense. They had strapped me down and taken whatever they wanted. I narrowed my eyes. What made her so special?

Mason's deep breath told me I wasn't going to like whatever he had to say. And I was correct.

"Dahlia is Naahir's daughter. But she's on our side," he assured me.

Naahir's daughter? I looked back at the dark-haired beauty and naturally began looking for physical similarities between them. At first, I found nothing that reminded me of her maniac of a father until we made eye contact. It was in the eyes. Her gaze was warm right then, but I could easily see how dark and hard they could become.

"Our side?" I asked Mason. *"What about you? You volunteered for this."*

"I did. And I want to see it through. But I don't trust them. Especially Dr. Young and Naahir. And what they've done to you... I can't let that happen again."

"You trust her?"

"I do."

My shoulders slumped with the realization that I had once again made a mess of things. He'd come here of his own free will, and I'd stormed the castle like a knight saving the damsel in distress.

I looked over Mason, at his clean clothes and fairly healthy parlor. He had a nice room with a comfortable bed. A quick glance told me he had a small kitchen and bathroom. His door wasn't locked from the outside. It wasn't even shut all the way. Mason was no damsel, and he didn't need to be saved. Especially by me. I ended up being the one who needed to be rescued. And all those others...

"There are others," I signed, my eyes closing from sheer exhaustion. *"We have to help them."*

"Others?" "What others?" Dahlia and Mason spoke at the same time.

I told them about the other "patients" I'd seen while searching for Mason. When I mentioned the flesh-eaters, both Dahlia and Mason tensed. By the time I finished, my body had had enough. Giving in, I laid back against the pillows with a sigh. My head was pounding.

"This is not good," Dahlia said. "You're right, Jane, we have to help those people. I'll talk to Dr. Chadwick. He wouldn't have agreed to this."

My eyes popped open and I pinned Dahlia with a look of panic. *"He's the one,"* I signed quickly. *"Don't trust him."*

"He's the one?" Her gaze narrowed, but my eyelids were already closing again. I shivered and blindly reached for a blanket, but Mason still sat on the edge of the bed.

"Here, let me help you," he said, pulling the sheets from under me. "Are you all right, Jane? Dahlia, something is wrong."

"I'm okay."

"The hell you are!"

I didn't want to do this, but Mason deserved to know. For his own safety, I reached across my body to unravel the bandage on my arm.

"What are you doing—"

Mason's words cut off abruptly as the binding came away, revealing the hidden wound. A heavy silence sucked the air out of the room. I didn't want to see his reaction, yet at the same time, I needed to.

Rocking back on his heels, his gaze locked on my arm. His expression was nothing short of horror-stricken, which slowly morphed into despair.

"Jane, may I examine you?" I started at the sound of Dahlia's voice being so close. She stood beside Mason, but somehow I hadn't noticed her.

"May I?" she asked again.

Weak and not really caring about anything but sleep at this point, I closed my eyes and nodded.

Cool fingers touched the edges of the wound. "How long ago were you bitten?"

I shook my head, unable to track the time. Instead, I pointed to the loose bandage under my arm. *"I came here right after."*

"Who dressed the wound?" she asked.

"Doctor Young."

"Doctor Young did this?" The disbelief in Mason's voice earned a glare from me.

"And Doctor Chadwick," I told them.

"On purpose?"

Sighing, I gave him a single nod, turning my attention back to Dahlia. Her brows had furrowed as she stared at the bite mark.

"What's wrong?" I asked.

She shook her head. "Nothing. Except, if I've gotten the timeline right, you were bitten within the last twenty-four hours. It should still look fresh."

We all looked down at the wound. Expecting to see torn skin, I tilted my head to the side, confused at the large circular scab.

"It looks like mine before it healed up." Mason lifted his shirt, and at first, all I could focus on was his lean, muscular torso. But as my hungry gaze devoured his chest, it landed on a circular white scar, and it suddenly became hard to breathe.

"Except mine didn't heal as fast," he said.

Dahlia nodded. "And my scar looks similar. I'd show you, but it's on my calf and I'm afraid I might fall over if I tried. I believe you've been given the cure, Jane." She placed the back of her hand on my forehead. "As soon as your fever breaks, we'll know if you're out of the woods."

As Dahlia leaned away, Mason reached for my hand. "Does this mean she's cured?"

"I don't know. Only time will tell. If it's okay, Jane, I'd like to examine you some more. Just to be sure there are no serious injuries. I'll be quick." From the signs of exhaustion lining her face, I knew she was telling the truth.

"Do you want Mason to leave?"

I shook my head no, and she began looking over the bruises on my arms.

"They've been taking plasma. A lot of it," Dahlia stated.

"Bone marrow, too," I informed them.

"Jane, we're going to roll you over now and check the incisions. Mason, I'm going to need your help. I don't have the strength."

As she examined my lower back, the sudden memory hit me hard, filling my eyes with tears. By the time Mason and Dahlia had turned me back around, I was shaking. At least the intense pain from the procedure had vanished now, leaving behind only a slight discomfort.

"That's a rough procedure," Dahlia said, her voice concerned. "But the incisions seem to be healing well, at least."

I pressed my lips together, not willing to discuss it. The quicker I could put everything behind me, the better.

"Goddamnit!" Mason exclaimed.

He paced next to the bed, running his hand through his hair. He'd been silent during the exam, but I'd seen the lines around his mouth deepen with each mark revealed.

He leaned over me with a frown. "I'm so sorry, Jane."

"Not your fault." If it was anyone's fault besides those bastards who did this to me, it was mine. I shouldn't have come. At least not alone. Kaden's face twisted in anger came to mind, and I almost smiled. I missed him.

Probably knowing exactly what I was thinking, Mason opened his mouth to argue but thought better of it. Instead, he turned to Dahlia. "Will she be okay?"

She nodded. "Only time will tell with the bite, but

otherwise, I'm diagnosing her with extreme exhaustion. That fever isn't helping either."

"Both of you need rest," Mason said, taking in the way Dahlia's shoulders had slumped. "We can discuss what we're going to do after we've all gotten some sleep."

"I agree," she replied.

Relieved, I let my eyes closed once more, but listened as Mason helped Dahlia stand. "Come on, I'll help you to your room."

Moments later, Mason came back, closing the door shut behind him. Seconds after the light dimmed behind my eyelids, his warm body slid in next to me.

"I want to hold you, but I don't want to hurt you," he whispered.

I wanted him to hold me too. A little discomfort wasn't going to stop me. I burrowed my face into his chest and sighed when his arms wrapped around me. I finally felt safe.

10
―――――

Stepping out of a tiny shower stall, I clutched the metal grab bar more as a precaution. My legs were stronger, and the aches and pains in my body had diminished considerably. A few hours of sleep and a hot shower was all it had taken for me to feel more human than I had in weeks.

Clean and clear-headed, I was ready to face reality. I wanted to escape this hell hole, walk right out and take Mason with me. As well as the other *test subjects*. I thought the words with gritted teeth. But it wasn't that simple. Mason thought he was doing something good, saving humanity. Though I could see his point, I also knew these people would end up doing more bad than good. And if we didn't leave soon, we were going to end up dead. Or worse, stuck here as lab rats for the rest of our lives.

However, convincing Mason wasn't going to be easy. He trusted Dahlia. And she hadn't done or said anything so far that would sway him. I had to admit, she came off as someone worthy of his trust.

I'd woken earlier to the sound of Mason and

Dahlia's soft voices and murmured plans. When Dahlia asked me to join the conversation, I suggested that Mason and I leave as soon as possible. As expected, Mason was not ready to jump ship, or cave, in this case. Though, he was all for getting me out unseen. I, however, had not been keen on this idea. And still wasn't.

We also still had the huge problem of what to do about the other unwilling patients. Though Dahlia and Mason both pointed out that we had no proof they weren't willing, we all agreed it had to be looked into. What was done to me was so unethical that it wasn't such a hard stretch to think they might do the same to others.

Dahlia, being the only one of us who had the authorization to move throughout the facility with ease, had taken on the task of finding out exactly what was going on. She blamed Dr. Chadwick and Dr. Young, claiming the need to save humanity had caused them to take extreme actions. Just like her father, Naahir, had when he'd threatened Mason into volunteering his immune blood.

I wasn't convinced. There was no way I could believe they cared about anyone but themselves. Not after what they'd done to me. But I'd kept my opinions to myself.

"Hey, feeling better?"

I jumped slightly, pulling my towel tighter around my chest. Mason leaned against the door jam, his arms crossed and his postured relaxed.

"You scared me," I signed, frowning.

"Sorry. I got worried when you didn't respond to my knock."

Mason's gaze swept over my half-naked body, igniting fires in its wake. Surprised at my body's response, I sucked in a sharp breath. The eyes that met mine reflected my own heated desire.

"Where's Dahlia?" I asked with shaky hands.

"Not here," was all he said before stepping into my personal space. My head tilted back to keep eye contact. I'd never tell him or Kaden this, but I loved it when they stood over me, looking down. I loved feeling small, and yes, a tad helpless. I hated that I loved it so much.

"I don't want to hurt you, but if I'm not inside of you soon, I won't be responsible for my actions."

I narrowed my eyes, holding back a smirk as I signed, *"And what actions would those be?"*

"You don't want to know," he replied without menace. "The begging and sniveling would be humiliating. Don't push me."

"You think I'd beg?" I asked, raising my eyebrows.

"Of course not. I was talking about myself."

Unable to hold back a smile, I shook my head. I loved how he could wind me up. As he chuckled, I took my revenge. A flick of a finger had my towel falling to the floor. Mason's laughter ceased.

Eyes suddenly heavy-lidded, Mason's muscles went taut.

Remembering how thin and bruised I looked, I began to second-guess myself. *"I'm not a hundred percent—"*

"I'll be gentle," he reassured. Not that I ever doubted him. And he proved it by lifting me carefully in his arms and carrying me to the bed.

Once he laid me down, Mason stood next to the bed, gazing down at me. I showed him everything I could with a single expression. I loved him, and I wanted him. I allowed myself to bask in desire, letting go of past hurts. None of it mattered. Not now.

Mason's lips tilted in a grin before he began taking off his clothes. With each slice of flesh revealed, my yearning for him grew. His gaze lowered to my heaving chest, then down to where I'd already parted my knees for him.

When he pulled a condom from a drawer next to the bed, his cheeks flushed red, though his gaze stayed dark with lust.

"I stole them from one of the exam rooms. Figured we might need them when I got back."

I shook my head in fake reproach, then smiled and opened my arms for him. Grinning back, he knelt on the bed to rain hot, open-mouthed kisses over my skin, starting with my neck and ending at my knees. I writhed, burning from his delicate touch, so crazy for him that by the time he came back up to kiss me full on the lips, I'd practically gone feral.

I buried my fingers in his hair and pulled, needing him closer.

"I missed your taste," he murmured against my mouth, his words driving me even crazier. "I love you so much, Jane."

In return, I showed him, without words, how I felt. I held him tightly, arching my back as he entered me. Ignoring the tingle of pain in my sore back, I encourage him to go deeper, loving him with my lips, teeth, and tongue, until the slide of his cock was so smooth he filled me completely.

I slid my hands down his chest as he sat up on his knees. Still deep inside me, he brought his thumb to my clit and began making slow circles while pulsing his cock in the same rhythm. As my eyes rolled back in my head, he gave a low chuckle full of masculine pride. If it hadn't felt so good, I might have slapped him. Then again, the man deserved the ego boost. Whatever he was doing to my body had me forgetting how sore I was. It had me forgetting everything but him. Which was exactly what I'd been hoping for.

"We fit perfectly," he groaned. "You're so beautiful, Jane. I can't hold out much longer. I've gone too long without you."

His low voice set me off and had my entire body stiffening as my climax overtook me.

"Yes," he groaned. "That's it, Jane." Voice strained, his thrusts became erratic until he too was overcome with his own release.

We stayed wrapped around each other as our breath slowly evened until I became aware of Mason's hand running lightly up and down my back. I sighed, snuggling deeper into his chest to breathe in his scent.

The peaceful moment only lasted a few moments. Then a heavy dose of guilt slammed into me.

Feeling me stiffen, Mason leaned back to look at my face. "What is it?"

So many things, I wanted to say. Here we were, getting lost in one another, making love when there were people suffering nearby. And for a moment I'd forgotten about Kaden. How could I have? He was probably taking turns cursing me out and worrying to death. God, I was such a bitch. If he forgave me, he was an idiot.

"Jane?" When I wouldn't meet his eyes, he sighed. "Is it Kaden?"

Surprised he picked up on my thoughts, I met his questioning gaze.

"I was so worried that I all I cared about was having you safe and in my arms. I should have asked before, but you needed rest." He paused and his eyes narrowed when

I dropped my head. "How did you get here? Where is Kaden?"

I rolled onto my back to stare at the ceiling and free my hands. *"He didn't come with me."*

Mason hesitated, then asked, "Where is he?"

"I don't know."

"What did you do?" The teasing in his voice was light, but I could hear the worry underneath.

"We were all together. Annabelle, Aidan, me, and Kaden, searching for you. I found a back way in and went alone."

"So they don't know you're here?"

I shook my head no.

"Damn it, Jane!" He sat up and ran a hand through his hair. It was getting long, the ends touching his shoulders.

I sat up next to him and pulled the sheet over my breasts as I watched him gritting his teeth at me.

"Kaden is probably worried and pissed as hell," he said. "I know I would be."

No probably about it. He would be angry, more than that. I expected the two of us were over. It was something I'd thought about off and on since I'd been captured. I remembered the anger and hurt I'd held onto, punishing him with my indifferent and sometimes petulant moods. Had I also been punishing him by finding the hidden entrance to the CDC and going in alone? I hadn't thought so at the time. I'd thought I was keeping him safe. Now I wasn't so sure. I'd never seen myself as a vindictive person, but my actions disappointed me, to say the least.

"Shit," Mason muttered as he slid off the bed and reached for his sweatpants.

"Where are you going?"

"To find some way to get a message to him," he said, pulling on a t-shirt.

"How?"

"I'm not sure, but maybe Dahlia knows."

He turned to leave but stopped at the door. Without turning around, he said, "I won't be long. You'll be safe here."

I slumped against the pillows. Another person was pissed at me, the story of my life.

Annabelle was probably having a fit. If I ever got out of here, I'd be lucky to have anyone left. I'd be alone again. I'd done it before. I could do it again. But when I tried to think of my life before Kaden and Mason, or even Annabelle and Aidan, my stomach ached at the bleak memories.

As the dark thoughts began to take over, I didn't realize at first that I was shaking. A sharp tingle zipped up my spine, then the back of my head slammed into the headboard as my whole body began to convulse.

"We're just in time. Bring the gurney."

Two hard hands pressed down on my shoulders as my body shook uncontrollably. Then as quickly as it came, the seizure stopped and I lay limp. I blinked open my eyes to see Dr. Chadwick leaning over me. My pulse leaped in fear at his empty expression.

For the first time since I'd laid eyes on him, he spoke directly to me. "Don't worry, Jane. We'll take care of you."

No. no, no, no, no, no. This couldn't be happening. Not again. *Mason!*

I must have mouthed his name because when Dr. Young came into view her grin was full of satisfaction. "Mason is a little busy right now. But don't worry. As Doctor Chadwick said, we'll take good care of you." Her eyes flashed, letting me know I wouldn't like her idea of taking care of me.

Dr. Young stepped back, then there was a flurry of activity as I was wheeled out of Mason's room.

I tried to fight, punching and kicking whoever came close enough, but they easily subdued me, holding me down and strapping my wrists and ankles to the gurney. Tears of anger, frustration, and fear blurred my vision, and I eventually gave up, exhausted.

When my body went lax, silence descended and the gurney came to a stop. Dr. Chadwick leaned over me once more, and I was suddenly blinded by a pin light. The light went off and his face disappeared, but not before I witnessed the faintest hint of a smile on his lips.

"Subject shows no signs of abnormalities. Phase three is a success. Let's proceed."

I closed my eyes in dismay, keeping them closed as they took my vitals as well as a gallon of blood. Not really, but the soreness in my arms and lethargic feeling in my limbs made me want to sleep.

Fighting off the feeling, I opened my eyes and winced as a bright light assaulted my pupils. Through the veil of my lashes, I was greeted by the familiar expanse of white upon white. They'd brought me back to my old room. Or one similar, anyway.

Licking my lips, I winced once more as I tried to swallow. My mouth was as dry as the desert. And there was a metallic taste lingering from when I'd bitten my tongue during the seizure.

My eyes fluttered shut once more. There was no reason to fight sleep and take what little peace I could find. Soon enough there'd be no more peace. They'd taken blood and run tests, but there would be more, no doubt. While they had poked and prodded, I'd let my mind wander, doing my best to hide from the pain and humiliation. But through the fog of numbness, I remembered Dr. Chadwick's declaration. Phase three had been successful. Did that mean I wouldn't be turning into a flesh-eater? If so, what did that mean for me? What did they need me for now?

The door opened and Dr. Chadwick came into the room with two female nurses following him. I hadn't even noticed he'd left. He gave me a fleeting look before dropping his gaze to the tablet in his hand.

"Is the subject ready?" he asked.

A nurse came to my side and fiddle with the monitor next to the bed. The beeping indicated my heart rate had increased, but either no one noticed, or they didn't care.

"Ready," she told him.

As Dr. Chadwick tapped something on the screen of his tablet, my gaze fixed on the glass doors and people walking into the room. Dr. Young opened the door and motioned for the woman behind her to enter. My mouth dropped open in horror as Annabelle stepped into the room, escorted in by an armed guard dressed in military fatigues.

Wrists imprisoned with nylon cable ties in front of her, she looked pissed. Her shoulders were pushed back, and her chin was so high, I wondered how she could see anyone over her nose. Then her eyes swept the room and they froze on me. Her chin dropped, and her eyes widened, giving me the perfect view of her split lip.

At the site of the wound, my gaze narrowed, and I took a good look at my disheveled friend. When I'd first realized she was there, fear like I'd never felt sped through me. I couldn't stand the thought of her in the hands of these monsters. But after seeing the blood on her lip and the fresh tears in her shirt, something new ran through me. Something much more primal. Annabelle was here, that meant something. And these assholes were going to die. Even if I had to die with them.

I thought she would say something, but Annabelle only pressed her lips together. When she winced, I ground my teeth together. Her gaze dropped to my balled fist, and she smirked before glaring at Dr. Young.

Dr. Young narrowed her eyes at Annabelle, then pushed her toward the bed. "Subject H56001 is ready," she said to a scowling Dr. Chadwick.

"Why isn't the subject prepared? I expected her to be on a bed with an IV in place. We don't know what to expect."

Dr. Young grimaced. "There were some… problems with the subject."

"Such as?"

She sighed. "She was much more difficult than we'd hoped. And on our time frame, I thought it best just to bring her straight here."

During their conversation, I'd been staring at Annabelle, hoping to figure out a way for us to communicate secretly. But when my friend's smirk broadened, I looked at Dr. Young for the first time and had to hold back a smile of my own. A brand-new shiner, already turning a lovely shade of purple, was blooming around her left eye. It was going to be a beauty.

Dr. Chadwick's sigh was long and dramatic. "I would like the experiment to be as organic as possible. But if this doesn't work, we'll extract a saliva sample. Proceed," he said, his attention back on the tablet.

The guard stepped back but didn't leave the room, his

gaze stuck to Anabelle like glue while Dr. Young pushed my friend closer to the bed.

"Open your mouth," she said to me. When I refused, she gripped my bottom jaw and forced it open. Pain spread through the lower half of my face, and I fought her grip as best I could.

"Stop! What are you doing to her?" Annabelle shouted as the other nurse pressed on my forehead to keep my head from thrashing back and forth.

I couldn't see from the two women standing over me, but I could hear a rustling sound and Anabelle hissing. "What the hell? Hey, stop! Ouch!" she yelled just before a small boney wrist was shoved in my face.

"Bite," Dr. Young said, and my struggles came to a sudden halt. *What the hell?*

Confusion mixed with sheer horror had me spacing out. In fact, the entire room was silent, still, like everyone was holding their breath. Then I snapped out of it and renewed my struggles two-fold. The hands holding my head slipped and I twisted away, dislodging the other nurse's grip on my jaw.

Dr. Chadwick gave a disapproving murmur. "This isn't going to work," he said just as Dr. Young shouted. "Hold her!" Though there was no need for her to yell, the nurses had not given up, and without the use of my hands, I was no match for them.

Then the lights went out and all hell broke loose. Or so it seemed.

Muffled curses and the clatter of something metal hitting the floor made me jump. The nurse to my left gave a surprised scream, then the hands holding my head and jaw were suddenly gone.

The room had turned pitch black. I couldn't see a

thing. All I could do was listen to the shoes squeaking against the tile floor as the owners rushed out of the room.

There was another crash, then a single male grunt before everything went dead silent. Even the machines next to the bed were no longer beeping, though the sound of my heart pounding beneath my ribcage was loud enough for anyone in the room to hear.

A hand landed gently on my arm and I instinctively jerked away.

"Shh, Jane, it's okay."

Shaking, I gaped silently. *Kaden?*

Cupping my cheek, he murmured soothing words into my ear. I couldn't see him, but I could feel him, hear his voice. Was he really there?

"We're here, Jane. We're going to get you out."

Out. We were getting out. The thought was almost unbelievable. He couldn't be here. This wasn't possible. I'd given up hope.

11

___

KADEN PROVED THAT HE WAS INDEED THERE TO GET ME out by pulling the wires and needles from my skin and helping me out of bed. I stood in front of him on shaky legs, wanting to reach out and hold onto him. But after everything, I was unsure of my place with him. Instead, I used the bed to find my balance as Kaden helped me into a pair of sweatpants. He slid them over my hips under the hospital gown then pulled the drawstring to tighten them.

I lifted my arms when he asked, and he whisked the gown off, quickly replacing it with a soft cotton t-shirt. Immediately, I felt warmer.

The shadows suddenly lessened as the emergency lights in the corridor came on. Though dim, they were just bright enough for me to see Kaden's face. He was also close. So close our noses almost touched.

His dark gaze collided with mine and I sucked in a breath and held it. Kaden could be hard to read at times. He held his emotions close, something I understood all too well. But in this one look, he'd given me everything. Hurt, anger, worry, fear…. A lot of fear. It was all bundled into one expression so intense that when he finally looked away I swayed on my feet.

"Come on," Kaden whispered, taking my arm and leading me from the room. "Aidan's cut the power, but they have a backup system for their locks. We don't have much time before they come back online."

Looking around the room, I took in the mess. Trays and instruments littered the floor, along with the body of the guard who'd brought in Anabelle. He was face down next to the door and not moving. Thinking of Anabelle...

Kaden, noticing my puzzled expression, nodded ahead of us. "She's right outside."

"*Where are the doctors?*" I signed.

Expression growing cold, he looked away from me. "With Annabelle."

No longer tired, adrenaline had taken over and I followed Kaden, doing my best to keep up. He pulled a gun from his side holster and wrapped his other hand around my upper arm, just above my elbow. Though he didn't tug when I fell back, it still felt odd to be handled that way.

Noticing my stiff posture, Kaden grasped my hand instead. "Don't want to lose you again," he murmured, and I relaxed.

Annabelle met us at the end of the hall. Her bow was slung across her back, and I almost smiled at the sight. Until my attention moved to the two people sitting against the wall, arms twisted behind them uncomfortably.

As Kaden and I approached, both looked up with matching scowls. I hesitated. I couldn't help it. Just the sight of their faces caused me to freeze up with irrational fear.

"It's okay, Jane," Kaden murmured. "It's over."

Swallowing, I nodded, but it didn't make the steps we took any easier.

Dr. Young smiled, that nasty, evil smile I'd grown used to, and something in me snapped. My kick landed hard on her stomach. Barefoot and as weak as I was, it couldn't have been my best effort, but I heard the pleasing sound of air whooshing from her lungs. Then she leaned over with a groan, and I had to refrain from hitting her again.

"You'll regret that," she said hoarsely.

"Shut up," Annabelle said, yanking the doctor to her feet. "Before I give you another makeover. You could use a little color on your right eye."

As I turned my attention to Dr. Chadwick, his eyes widened in fear, but from the look of things, I wouldn't need to kick his ass. Someone had already done it for me. Blood ran down his chin from a split lip, but that wasn't the worst of his injuries. Half his face looked like someone had slammed him one too many times into a brick wall.

I signed one-handed, not willing to let go of Kaden. *He must have put up a fight.*

"No," was all Kaden said. "Come on, let's get out of here."

Unfortunately, he had to let go of my hand to grab Dr. Chadwick by the arm and pull him to his feet. The two doctors stumbled along at our fast pace but thankfully kept quiet.

Kaden seemed to know where he was going, and we slipped through the unlocked steel doors easily. A shout rang out in the distance, followed by the distinct sound of multiple pairs of boots stomping over the tile floor.

"Hey!" Dr. Young suddenly yelled out. "Hey, over here!"

"Shit." Annabelle slapped a hand over the doctor's

mouth, but it was too late. They were headed straight for us.

Frantic for a place to hide, my gaze landed on a door several feet away.

"There," Kaden said, seeing it at the same time.

"We won't make it," Annabelle said.

"Stop, now!" "Drop your weapons!" The commands came from behind us, but it wasn't the armed guards that had me suddenly freezing in place.

The seconds that followed happened quickly, but in my memory, time had slowed so that every single detail had been embedded.

Kaden opened the sealed door, his head facing the other end of the hallway, watching for the guards. So, by the time he recognized what was on the other side of the door, it was too late.

The sound of hundreds, if not thousands of clattering teeth echoed throughout the corridor, sending a shiver down my spine.

Eyes widening, Kaden shoved at the door, but the flesh-eaters were already pushing their way through.

"Run!" he yelled at us, shoving Dr. Chadwick out of the way at the same time the guards reached us, blocking our only escape.

I barely paid them any mind though, my attention claimed by the sight of Dr. Chadwick tripping over his own feet. Kaden instinctively reached out to help him, but a couple of flesh-eaters lurched into them. Kaden pulled out of one's grasp, and I grabbed his hand and yanked, just as the doctor's screams suddenly cut off.

Unable to look, I turned away from the feeding frenzy and found Annabelle trying to pull a defiant Dr. Young to safety. She ignored our pleas, kicking Annabelle in the shin. As my friend let go, the doctor stumbled back with a triumphant smile, and I shook my head at her idiocy. The flesh-eaters were practically on top of us.

"Come on!" Kaden yelled, pulling at Annabelle as the guards I'd forgotten about opened fire on the flesh-eaters. I flinched, covering one ear, but didn't stop running.

At the end of the hall, Kaden swung open the door. I took one last look over my shoulder and wished I hadn't. The corridor had filled with flesh-eaters, and I no longer could see the guards or Dr. Young.

"Come on," Annabelle said, hurrying me into the next hallway. When she didn't follow, I grabbed her hand, but she shook me off. "Just a minute," she said while reaching for a small red and white box on the wall. She pulled down the lever on the fire alarm, then slipped back out the door, slamming it shut behind her.

I'd expected the alarm to sound and had covered my ears in preparation, but nothing happened.

"Jane, come on," Kaden said, gripping my hand again and giving it a tug. I too felt the urgency to keep running. The flesh-eaters might have been trapped on the other side of that door, but they were still too close for comfort.

We continued at a fast pace until I had to stop. I placed a hand on Kaden's arm, asking for a rest. I had to bend over to catch my breath. Something that wouldn't have happened a few weeks ago. Or however long I'd been in this awful place. I would have asked, but finding out the answer terrified me more than not knowing.

Annabelle paced a few feet away, her boots coming into view then leaving again. When I stood upright, Annabelle stopped. "Are you okay?" she asked.

I nodded. I wasn't a hundred percent, but I would live.

For now. The white bandage wrapped around my arm stood out like a beacon. I closed my eyes.

"Jane?" Kaden said from beside me.

His hand hovered over my bandage, his fingers curled inward as though he were holding back from ripping it off. Instead, he dropped his arm to his side and brought his fearful gaze to mine.

"Oh my God, Jane!" Annabelle cried, rushing at me. Unlike Kaden, she had no qualms about lifting my arm.

Except for Annabelle's hands, they both held still as she unraveled the white gauze. I held my breath along with them, wondering what we'd find. It no longer hurt. In fact, now that I was thinking about it, my arm felt perfectly fine.

"It's fine," I tried to tell them one handed. They ignored me, of course, to see for themselves.

When the last section of gauze fell away, I think they were shocked to see it healing as well as it was. It looked almost the same as it had when Dahlia and Mason had examined it, a circle of healing scabs. Though it looked less red and swollen than it had before.

"You're…"

"Fine," I answered Annabelle while pulling my arm from her grasp.

"I told you. It's okay. I'm not infected," I signed, wondering if that last sentence had been a lie. The wound healed, yes, but what happened after the seizure confused me. Why had they wanted me to bite Annabelle?

I looked up at my friend to see her worried expression smoothing out. Mine, on the other hand, only deepened. Was I really cured? Only time would tell. What was most important now was getting weapons. I'd felt naked ever since my knives had been taken away, and if we were going to get out of here, I was going to need a way to protect myself.

Next to me, Kaden let out a long breath of air, turning his back to me, and I suddenly forgot about the weapons. His back rose and fell with each deep breath, and I itched to reach out. I wanted to rub my hands up and down his back, comforting him. I was glad I hadn't. Because two breaths later, he swung around, fire in his eyes.

"Why, Jane?" he snapped. "What was going through your mind? What made you think coming here alone was the best option?"

Those are good questions, was my immediate thought. Ones I'd asked myself time and time again. Why had I left him? Why lie and go alone?

I lifted a hand and dropped it, before lifting both. *"I don't know."*

He jerked back as though I'd hit him, and I flinched.

Brows lifted to his hairline, his mouth dropped opened. "You don't know? You put yourself in danger for no reason? Lied to us, left us… left me, for absolutely no reason at all?"

I shook my head. I hadn't meant it that way. But it was so hard to put into words.

I took a deep breath before trying again. *"No. I thought I was keeping you safe. But that's not the only reason. I just don't know what that reason is. I'm sorry."*

Kaden shook his head with a snort, turning his head as though he couldn't stand to look at me. I watched him closely, at the way he licked his lips, a sign of agitation I'd never seen him do before. His fists clenched at his sides, and his neck tightened with tension. Little veins that popped up near his temples, throbbing in the rhythm of his pulse.

72

He finally faced me again, and I had to blink away tears. I'd hurt him so badly. Whether our relationship survived or not, the guilt would follow me for the rest of my life.

"I know why," he said, his voice sounding defeated. "It was revenge. Punishment for leaving you first."

I began to shake my head, but he continued, his words halting my denial.

"It might not have been the only reason," he conceded. "But don't deny it crossed your mind. You wanted to prove that you didn't need me. That you could save Mason by yourself. But the thing is, I already knew that. I already know you don't need me."

Again, I began to protest when he thumped his chest with the flat of his palm. "Not like I need you," he said. "I've apologized a hundred times, but I won't continue to do so. Either you forgive me or we get out of here and go our separate ways. I've lived without you. Before I met you and again when I left with Mason and Naahir. I know what's it's like without you. It's lonely and bleak, and I'm terrified to go back to that. But I will if I have to."

Already astounded by his words, it staggered me to hear him admit he was terrified. And about being without me, no less. I was without words. I didn't know how to respond. It was the exact same way for me. I just hadn't been able to admit it.

"I need you, Jane," he said again, placing a shaking hand on my cheek.

I leaned into him, savoring the warmth of his touch and hoping it wasn't the last time I felt it.

"But if you don't need me, I'll walk away."

I shook my head, frowning when he pulled his hand away. I grabbed it and brought it back to my cheek, patting it once so he'd know not to move. His lips tilted slightly, and when I let go, he stayed.

"I do need you," I signed. *"I was stupid and reckless."*

"I agree," he said.

Annabelle snorted, and I jumped, having forgotten she was there. I turned apoplectic eyes on her. I hated airing out my dirty laundry, but I especially hated that she'd had to sit through all of that.

"Don't worry about it," she said, waving a hand. "But you should hurry this along. Kiss and make up, or whatever you're going to do, because we have to go.

Kaden took a step back. "She's right, we should go."

"No," I signed. *"Don't walk away."*

"We have to go, Jane."

"I need you," I pleaded with my eyes. *"Don't leave me."*

"Shh," he said, cupping my cheek once more. He bent at the waist and lifted my chin, whispering his next words against my trembling lips. "I won't leave you, Jane. I promise."

Then he kissed me and the world fell away. Nothing, not him leaving or me risking my life, or this damned underground horror of a hospital, meant anything anymore. Annabelle was gone, my body no longer hurt, and I was floating, lost in him. In Kaden.

His tongue traced the seam of my lips. They parted for him without contest. His chest rumbled appreciatively under my palm, and I realized I'd plastered myself to him. My fingers were clinging to his shirt and my leg had hitched over his left hip. But I wasn't embarrassed. I wanted him, and I need him. And he needed to know just how much.

"Jane. Kaden. Guys!"

We heard her, but both of us were slow to act. Too

caught up in each other to pay attention to our surroundings. A stupid move on our parts. Extremely stupid.

"How touching."

Kaden's lips left me so abruptly I almost stumbled back. Once steady, I swung around to face what I'd already guessed. I should have been glad it was just Naahir and his men who had snuck up on us and not the flesh-eaters, but with a gun pointed at my face, I was far from grateful.

"Jane, what a surprise. We were just coming for you." Naahir smiled as he cocked the hammer of the gun. An unnecessary move as it was a double-action revolver. If I hadn't been so scared, I would have rolled my eyes at the dramatics.

"I'm sorry," Annabelle said, being held by one of Naahir's men. "I didn't hear them until it was too late."

"Kaden," Naahir said, his eyes still on mine. "Drop the gun and step back. Please," he tacked on.

I hadn't seen Kaden draw his gun. Surprised, I took my eyes off Naahir to stare at Kaden. He hesitated, but there were three armed soldiers behind Naahir, weapons at the ready. One held Annabelle. There was nothing either of us could do.

Kaden dropped his gun and kicked it to the side, near the wall, away from Naahir and his men. Naahir's grin widened knowingly, but he said nothing.

The feeling of being trapped overwhelmed me. Gasping for breath, I took a step back and bumped into Kaden. I stopped and leaned into him, his warmth allowing me to calm down and gather my strength.

"We just want Jane and we'll get out of your hair,"

Kaden said, his rumbling voice surprising me. That wasn't right. What about Mason?

"I'm sorry, but that's just not possible. Not anymore." Naahir's said with false regret. "See, she's become valuable to us now. I'm no doctor or scientist. But my daughter is. She's won awards, you know. And she tells me Jane is the key."

Dahlia told him that? When?

As Naahir spoke, Kaden stiffened next to me. "Key to what? The cure?" he asked.

His expression became amused. "Sure. The cure." He smirked. "Come on." He motioned for us to go first and the guards moved around us as we followed them down the dark corridor.

Though I tried to walk confidently, I started to shake, but it wasn't until Kaden wrapped his arm around my shoulders that I noticed the trembling. He pulled me tightly against him and I glanced back to check on Annabelle. She started to give me a smile when one of the guards gave her a little shove from behind.

"Don't fucking touch me, douche bag," she growled.

The soldier turned away, but not before I saw the corners of his lips tilt up just a tad. Stiffening, my gaze ran over him from head to toe and widened. He wore the same thick, green camouflage coat and pants as the other soldiers. Along with a matching hat that dipped low over his eyes. The rest of his face was cast in shadows, the dark corridor not giving enough light see his expression. Noticing me watching him, he scowled.

Kaden's arm tightened around my shoulders and I turned back, confused and little suspicious. But when I glanced at the man next to me for answers, his expression only tightened.

At the end of the corridor was a door, only this door was different than the ones I'd seen before. It was made of steel, but it looked thicker and harder to open than the others. My first thought was that something important must be inside.

"We're here," Naahir said from behind us, speaking into a two-way radio.

From in front of us, there was a hiss, like a release of pressure, then the heavy door swung open. We stepped inside, and I gave the room a wary glance before settling on two familiar faces. I tensed, crushing Kaden's hand in my constricting grip when I saw one of them held a two-way radio, identical to the one Naahir had spoken into. Betrayal sat heavily in my stomach, as cold fingers of dread crept up my spine.

12

———

UNLIKE THE GLOOMY HALLWAY, WE STEPPED INTO A brightly lit laboratory. In fact, it was so bright, I had to squint for a few seconds until my eyes could adjust. My first impression was that it was clean, organized, and held no odor. And it was as cold as a meat locker. I shivered as we moved toward the center of the large room, the tile floor almost painfully cold on my bare feet.

I was so far removed from medicine and science studies, that the equipment and machines were foreign to me. Plasma screens with text too far away to make sense, expensive looking microscopes, and a few filing cabinets were the only things I recognized. There were white-coated scientists moving around the edges of the room, paying no attention to us. I watched one of them for a moment as she drew pipettes of fluid from one tube and transferred it to another.

She looked up at me, making eye contact through her thick goggles before glancing over my shoulder. "Would you like some privacy, Doctor Khoury?"

"Yes, please. Give us a moment," she answered.

As she and the other scientists left the lab, using another exit in the back that I filed away for later, my attention switched to the soldiers who had followed us into the lab. At a flick of Naahir's wrist, one of them stepped back out into the hallway to stand guard, I presumed, while the other two stayed at our backs.

Feeling more prepared, I finally looked at the other two people in the room. Mason stood with his legs shoulder-width apart and his arms crossed, his posture defensive. Next to him, standing a little too close for my comfort, was a rigid looking Dahlia.

While Mason still wore the same gray sweats, Dahlia had changed into blue scrubs and a white lab coat. Her arms rested at her sides, one holding onto the radio, but her shoulders were tense and her lips were pursed into a tight line.

As my gaze moved over them both, something seemed different. At first, I thought it was Dahlia's wardrobe change, but the longer I stared, the more I noticed. The dark circles under her eyes were absent, as well as the sallow cheeks I remembered. She also hadn't coughed or hunched her shoulders once since we walked in. In fact, if I hadn't seen her just hours before, I would never have known she'd been sick.

Her brown eyes moved over us, stopping for a moment when they reached me. My own gaze narrowed, but she didn't show any signs of guilt for deceiving us, nor did she seem smug. In fact, she was all too composed.

"Kaden, this is my daughter, Dahlia," Naahir said as he strode towards her. She inclined her head, accepting his peck on the cheek. "You're looking better today," he told her.

"Father," she said, stiffly. She gave us a closed lip smile

and nodded. "Nice to meet you, Kaden. I've already met Jane and Mason," she said before glancing behind me. "You must be Annabelle. I've heard a lot about you."

My brows furrowed but smoothed out when I felt Naahir's gaze on me. "Jane," he said. "You have no idea how… helpful you have been. Without you, my daughter wouldn't have survived. For that, I owe you my life." Placing a hand over his heart, he bowed his head slightly.

I might have been shocked by his announcement, but I couldn't help but reply to his last comment. Kaden didn't want to let go of my hand, but after a tug, he finally acquiesced.

"And I'll gladly take it," I signed.

There was a snicker behind me, and Mason had to turn away to hide a smile. But I wasn't smiling. That hadn't been a joke. Not even close.

Naahir's grin fell as he eyed our little group, his brow lowering. "I can't read sign language, but I can guess your response. I'm sorry," he sighed regretfully, sounding so far from sincere it was laughable.

"Let me and my friends, including Mason, go, and we can call it even," I signed.

Kaden translated this time, and Naahir pursed his lips in thought. Slowly he shook his head no, sighing once more. "I'm sorry, again. I can't give you what you want. Not yet, anyway. You see, you're special, Jane. From what Doctor Chadwick has told me, his experiments have yielded better results than he'd hope for. Thanks to you."

He walked over to a long stainless steel table and patted one of two stools that stood next to it. "Please, Jane, come sit down and we can begin. The sooner we get this over with, the better. Annabelle, you as well, please."

Always so polite, I thought with a sneer. But my scoff

turned into a gape as Annabelle slid past me. She sat down on the stool as asked without question. Even Naahir's eyes narrowed at her willingness to comply.

Bemused, he gestured for me to follow suit. "Now, Jane."

I glanced at Kaden, but he stared straight ahead with no expression for me to decipher. Mason, Dahlia, and Annabelle's weren't any easier to read. No one spoke up or told me not to follow, or even asked why.

I shook my head and ground my teeth together. This was stupid. And confusing.

Not one to just follow like a dog on a leash, I stepped back but stopped when I almost ran into the soldier standing right next to me. The guard's cold stare made me shiver.

Pissed that I let it get to me, I turned my own glare on Naahir. *"Why?"* I asked.

Kaden translated in a stiff voice but said nothing else.

"Because you're the key to a new life, Jane," Naahir said, excitement lighting his voice. "Not only are you the antidote… You're also the disease."

I flinched at the word disease, and my mouth dropped open with the shock of his statement. What did he mean? I was a disease?

"You're a carrier, Jane. Or at least, we hope. Please, come sit down and we can determine if the tests are accurate."

The soldier at my back nudged my shoulder and I stumbled forward. Out of the corner of my eye, I saw Kaden turn swiftly, only to freeze when the soldier pointed his rifle at his chest. Jaw clenched, Kaden stepped back, but his dark gaze stayed glued to the guy as he nudged me again, this time much softer.

I sat on the stool and immediately glanced at Annabelle, but she refused to look at me. Unease settled heavy in my stomach. I was missing something. I looked at their faces again. Mason, Dahlia, Kaden, Anabelle, and… I looked at the soldiers. They all knew something, I decided. And had purposely kept me in the dark.

Once I had sat down, the soldier had moved away, leaving Anabelle and I separated from the group.

Naahir paced, then turned to Dahlia. "Where's Doctor Chadwick and Doctor Young? They should be here by now."

I stiffened at the mention of the doctors, surprised when Annabelle's small hand wrapped around one of mine and gave it a squeeze.

"They aren't coming," Dahlia said.

Naahir stopped pacing and went to stand in front of his daughter. "What do you mean?"

"I'm sorry, father," she whispered.

Still staring at Annabelle's hand, now gripping mine securely, I almost missed the chagrin in her voice. My head slowly lifted to see father and daughter staring at one another. A lone tear fell from one of Dahlia's eyes, and Naahir's shoulders tightened.

"I lied to you," she said.

"What do you mean—"

He didn't finish as with a nod of her head, the once immobile people in the room went into immediate action.

Something in Dahlia's expression must have thrown him off balance because Naahir didn't put up a fight when Mason took his gun and restrained him with a pair of handcuffs.

While Mason handled Naahir, Kaden had twirled on the soldier who had shoved me. He grabbed the soldier by the wrist and elbow, bringing him down to the floor and disarming all at once. Then a quick palm strike, the guy was out.

While Kaden's back was turned, the guard outside the door ran in, his rifle at his shoulder. I jumped from the stool, intent on helping Kaden, but Annabelle held me down.

"Just wait," she whispered as the third soldier, the one who had jostled Annabelle in the hallway, slammed his rifle into the guy's face. "My man's got this." Aidan looked up from the unconscious guard to give her a crooked smile.

With hair pushed up into his hat and a clean-shaven face, he really did look like a different person. It was unlikely, though, to have been enough to trick Naahir or the other soldiers.

"You too, Aidan?" Naahir said, confirming my suspicions. "I never would have thought you or your sister would betray me like this."

"I owe you nothing," Aidan said in a detached voice. "You're not my father. The only reason I hung around was for Dahlia's sake. She asked for my help."

"That's why you're here?" Naahir asked, eyebrows raised.

Aidan's gaze landed on Mason, Kaden, and me, before stopping on Annabelle. "Not entirely."

Enough was enough. Turning to Annabelle, I signed, my hands moving furiously.

"Wait, slow down, Jane. I don't understand," she said.

Gritting my teeth, I slowed down. *"Someone tell me what is going on. Right now."* My impatience caused me to sign in jerky movements, leaving Annabelle just as perplexed.

"What's going on," Dahlia answered for her, "is that

my father is an opportunist who will not be winning this one. Dad," she said, moving to face him, "I lied to you. From the moment I saw Jane, I knew what you were up to. I know part of you thinks you're helping, but experimenting on human beings is wrong."

"I just wanted to save you," he said.

Dahlia closed her eyes and shook her head lightly. "I wish that was true, but the evidence suggests otherwise." She gestured to me, though neither looked in my direction. "I'm well now, Dad. Can't you tell?" And it was obvious, if anyone looked, that she was no longer sick.

"And as I told Jane, I'm grateful. It's a miracle!" he exclaimed.

"It wasn't the tests on Jane that cured me," she snapped. "Mason's blood did that. What was given to Jane was a vaccine we'd been working on. And it worked. We can finally eradicate the flesh-eater virus."

I rocked back, shocked by this new information. The world was about to change again. My emotions ranged from excitement to fear of the unknown. But mostly relief. I wasn't sick.

"What was the plan, though?" Dahlia asked Naahir. "That's what I don't understand."

"Are you kidding me?" he yelled. "It would have been like having a living breathing flesh-eater at our command. The perfect weapon against humans and flesh-eaters alike," he said, sounding forlorn.

Anabelle snorted at the same time a scoff escaped Mason's lips. He'd been quiet up until that point. Everyone had as we'd listened to the father-daughter pair duke it out. Now that my attention had turned to him though, I couldn't help but run my eyes over his form. He looked perfect. Not a hair out of place. Though it had been mussed only hours before. My cheeks heated momentarily, remembering our time in bed together.

Mason happened to look over right at that moment and winked. I wasn't embarrassed at having been caught though. If we were in a different setting, I would have leaped into arms by now.

Mason had been holding onto Naahir's shoulder and when he'd snickered, Naahir turned to glare at him. "What are you laughing at?" he snapped.

"You, if you think you can control Jane. I guarantee your *weapon*," he sneered at the word, "would have turned on you the first chance she got."

"Not after we got through with her," Naahir said with a menacing grin.

Naahir suddenly staggered back, his head whipping around from the force of Mason's fist.

"Mason, no!" Dahlia placed a hand on Mason's arm, but he'd already taken a step back.

"I'm not going to hit him again," he said through a tense jaw.

"Not that he doesn't deserve it," Dahlia said, "but thank you."

As Dahlia called someone on the two-way radio about taking Naahir off our hands, Kaden came to stand next to me. He grabbed my hand and held onto it, though his attention stayed on the rest of the room.

"Come on, Dad," Dahlia said as four men, three in scrubs and one in fatigues, walked into the room. The rest of us braced for more trouble, but Dahlia shook her head. "My father only thought they were all following him."

"Sneaky, sneaky." Naahir smiled. "Like father, like daughter."

"Hardly," she said abruptly, as one of the men in

scrubs took her father's arm. The other men took care of the guards on the floor, easing them up on their feet. Both were only semi-conscious but alive.

"I want answers," I demanded as soon as they were gone.

Dahlia nodded. "And you deserve them. But first, you need clothes and shoes. It's too cold in here. And when was the last time you ate? Never mind." She waved a hand. "I have a feeling it's been too long."

When I began to argue, Annabelle placed a gentle hand on my shoulder. "Your lips are almost blue, Jane." She looked down at my feet and winced. "And your poor feet are probably ice cubes by now."

That was true. I curled my toes in reflexively and she smiled.

"I can hear your stomach from here," Mason ganged up on me, adding a wink that sped up my pulse.

Kaden didn't say anything, but he lifted me from the stool and into his arms, cradling me as he followed Dahlia out of the lab. The look on his face said any arguments from me would go unheard. But what he didn't know was that there was no way I was going to complain about being this close to him. I let my head rest on his shoulder and placed a hand over his chest, so I could feel his heartbeat beneath my palm.

As Mason walked beside us, he reached over and brushed his fingers gently over my cheek, and I closed my eyes to absorb the loving gesture. I wasn't sure where we would go from here, but being between them like this again felt like I was already home.

13

ONCE WARM AND FED, MY DEMAND FOR ANSWERS HAD softened, but I still felt on edge. Dahlia had taken us from the lab to a section that housed the staff. Including Mason. These rooms were more comfortable. Less hospital like and reminded me of college dorms. They had a fully staffed kitchen and cafeteria, but we opted to take our food to Dahlia's room. It was slightly bigger than Mason's and with more seating. I'd been forced to sit on the bed, however. Their mother-henning had earned them all an eye roll that they of course ignored.

After I'd eaten, Mason tried to get me to lie down, but I refused. If I did, I'd most likely fall asleep. That couldn't happen. If I slept now, I'd surely have nightmares. I refused to close my eyes again until we were safe. As cozy as everything seemed on the surface, my skin felt tight and jumpy. We needed to leave.

Not sure where to start, I rubbed my hands against my thighs and looked around the room. Kaden sat in a chair next to the bed, one hand on my back rubbing soothing circles. He now looked relaxed, yet watchful. Though, when he first placed a hand on my back and felt the ridges of my spine, he'd grimaced, then cursed, vowing to fatten me up as soon as we got home. I had to admit, that sounded good to me.

Mason sat at the bottom of the bed, one hand closed over my socked foot as he spoke quietly to Dahlia. She listened intently, her brows furrowed. I'd gotten the gist of their conversation, but it was something I was trying not to think about at the moment.

My attention snagged on Annabelle cuddled up with Aidan, and my eyes narrowed on the couple. Aidan brushed a strand of hair off her face and leaned over to press a kiss to the top of her head at the same moment his gaze collided with mine. I knew where to start.

"*Who are you?*" I signed at him. I'd thought I'd known our mysterious Aidan. As much as any of us could. I didn't trust easily, but he had earned that trust over and over again. I was disappointed to find out he'd been lying all this time.

As my hands moved, the room fell silent. Aiden wasn't as good at sign language as the others, but from his expression, he'd gotten the gist of what I'd asked. Brows furrowed, he pulled away from Annabelle, even as she protested, and took a deep breath.

"Jane," Annabelle began, but he cut her off.

"Naahir is my step-father," he told me. "He married my mother when she became pregnant with Dahlia. We never got along." Aidan looked over at his sister. "But I stuck around for Dahlia's sake."

The rest of the story he described was complicated. Naahir, though as sneaky and manipulative as he was, did care for Dahlia. And when she became sick, he went a little crazy. He'd been searching for Mason. Not Mason precisely, but a person like him, convinced there had to be people immune to the flesh-eaters. And he'd been right. But Dahlia knew her father and was afraid what lengths he'd go to get the cure.

Which brought us around to when we'd met Aidan all those months ago.

"Dahlia asked me to keep an eye on Naahir," he said. "I knew what he was capable of as well. Maybe more so." A pained look crossed his face, and Annabelle reached for his hand, biting her lip in concern. But whatever had caused such a reaction, he didn't divulge.

None of that explained why he was on our property, miles away from his stepfather. But from the way he looked at Annabelle, I had a feeling I knew the real reason.

"*Why did you come to us?*" I asked anyway.

He looked at Annabelle, and I had my answer, though he spoke it for me.

"I shouldn't have. But I had to keep her safe."

"But we hadn't met yet," Annabelle said.

His cheeks became suspiciously bright as he shrugged. "I saw you at my father's compound," he told her. "I can't explain it. I just needed to know you were safe."

Annabelle's eyes went dreamy, and I looked away, letting them have their moment in private. Knowing he'd lied to us was a hard pill to swallow, but deep down, I couldn't fault him. Dahlia was his sister. I would have done the same for the people I loved.

"*What about the rest of you?*" I signed. "*Start from the beginning. Tell me what happened after you left me, Mason.*"

He frowned hard, and I immediately regretted the way I'd formed that last sentence.

"*I didn't mean it that way,*" I tried.

"No, no. It's okay, Jane. I know you didn't. But I shouldn't have left you." There was a double meaning in both the intensity of his words and the pleading look in his eyes.

The grip on my foot tightened. "I'll regret leaving you for the rest of my life," he said. "And I promise I never will again."

Heart beating wildly at his declaration, I could barely take in a breath. Because I had a feeling he meant every word of that promise and yet, he was going to have to break it very soon, I was afraid.

"I'm just glad you were okay," he said with a smile, bringing us back to the present. "As you know, I was hoping to find a way to communicate with Kaden and the rest that you were with me. I mean, they had to be going crazy!"

"Oh, we were," Annabelle said. "I can't believe you did that to us, Jane," she chastised with a glared sent my way. "We'll have words later."

Sorry, I mouthed, then turned to Kaden. *"I'm sorry,"* I signed.

Kaden leaned in and placed a chaste kiss on my lips, his eyes sparkling down at me when he pulled away. "I know, Jane," he said, becoming serious. "We'll also talk about it later."

"I better be in on that conversation," Mason said, waggling his eyebrow and earning groans from around the room.

"Just get on with the story," cried Annabelle. "No offense, Dahlia, but I'm ready to get out of here."

Dahlia laughed. "None taken," she said, though her eyes looked sad.

"Okay, okay," Mason continued. "As I was saying, I

went searching for Dahlia because if she couldn't get someone else out there to find Kaden, I'd planned to go alone. And damn them if anyone tried to stop me. But as it turned out, they'd found us first.

"It was pure luck!" he exclaimed, looking at Dahlia. "Dahlia had been in the security office when the cameras spotted them. Since I pretty much talked non-stop about you guys, she'd known right away who they were and had welcomed them into the facility without Naahir and his guards noticing."

"It's true," she said. "The talking… non-stop."

We all laughed because it was so accurately Mason. He could be a talker.

"Doctor Young and Doctor Chadwick were another matter," she continued. This time no one laughed. "What they were doing to humans and flesh-eaters alike was nauseating. The experiments had gone beyond finding a cure or creating a vaccine."

I could visibly see the shudder run through her, but she refused to say more. It was not something I wanted to hear anyway. Not with my own torture still fresh in my mind.

"When we got back and you weren't in my room," Mason said to me, picking up the story, "we devised a plan to cut the power and rescue you."

"Doctor Chadwick and Doctor Young are dead," Kaden told them. "We were attacked by flesh-eaters and they didn't make it. We sealed off that section of the facility, but with the power cut, you'll want to make sure."

"I know," Dahlia said, and she didn't sound upset by this news one bit. "I was informed as soon as you pulled the fire alarm. We're taking care of it."

Something occurred to me then. Flesh-eaters were

dead. They were rotting bodies with snapping teeth and moving limbs. How could they become human again? And who would want to be brought back from that?

"We can cure them all?" I signed.

Dahlia frowned. "Unfortunately, no. The cure only works for the recently bitten. Once you turn, there's nothing that can be done."

I nodded. That made much more sense. This change, the healing of our world, was going to take time. It frightened, yet excited me.

As the conversation wound down, Dahlia suggested we rest before making our journey home, but I was the first to refuse. I stood from the bed, shaking my head before she could finish offering the use of the facility.

"I'm ready to get home," I signed to her. But I had a few more things on my mind. *"You'll take care of the other patients?"* I asked. I didn't have to explain.

"Yes," she said solemnly. "I have staff already looking them over. And I promise you, this will never happen again. Not while I'm heading up this facility."

"Home sounds good," Mason said, standing from the bed. "I'm going to my room to grab my things."

I watched Mason disappear before turning to Dahlia. Her gaze was already latched onto mine.

"You need him here, don't you?" I asked. When she said nothing, I raised a brow. *"Don't lie."*

She stuffed her hands in her pockets and sighed. "I think we have what we need."

"But having him here would help?"

"Yes, it would definitely help."

"Jane, what are you doing?" Kaden asked from behind me.

I looked over my shoulder and grimaced. He had to

be confused. It wasn't that long ago that I was angry at him and Mason for leaving me, and here I was about to tell one of them to leave again, or in this case, stay.

But I'd learned my lesson. They'd made some mistakes in the past. Maybe they shouldn't have stayed away so long, but they're reasoning had been sound. This was important. Humanity was more important than me wanting to be with the people I loved. No matter how much it killed me to do so, I had to let Mason go.

"Okay," I signed to Dahlia. It wasn't my decision, and Mason nor Dahlia needed my permission. But I felt like giving my blessing was necessary for my peace of mind. And Mason's.

Kaden dropped his head, looking back up with a tortured expression. "Don't do this," he pleaded.

Mason walked back into the room, his beat-up backpack in hand. "Don't do what?" he asked, slinging the pack over one shoulder. "Ready to go? It'll be getting dark soon."

"We have a place not far from here where we can stay until morning." This came from Annabelle who had been watching me quietly for a while now. She hadn't said a word about my exchange with Dahlia, but she didn't have to. Disapproval was written all over her face.

"Great," Mason said. "Jane, do you want me to carry you this time?" he lifted a brow, giving me a wicked look that almost changed my mind. Almost.

Biting my lip, I shook my head and pulled back my hand when he tried to take it.

"Jane?" he asked, all humor gone.

"You have to stay here," I signed.

"Why?"

Dahlia and I exchanged looks. "Mason," she began

cautiously, her gaze still accessing me. My chin wobbled but I nodded, letting her know she should continue.

Mason spun around. "No. I've done everything you've asked of me. You have your cure and a vaccine to boot."

"But it's still in the beginning stages. We have no idea how well they're going to work. We still need to test—"

"No." Mason's terse response was followed by a surprised silence.

Besides the pulse in his cheek as he ground his teeth together, Mason stood as still as a statue. I'd never seen him so angry, it baffled me. Wasn't this what he wanted? To help end this nightmare and hopefully bring our world back to the way it was? Or maybe even better? He'd left us for this.

"Are you saying the vaccine given to Jane might not work?" Kaden asked, clearly his mind going somewhere totally different. "What about the seizure? Should we be worried?"

The tight muscles in Dahlia's forehead relaxed. "No, no, please don't worry," she said, her tone apologetic. "I'm sorry. Jane should have no problems. The seizure was actually the pivotal moment. Her body fought the virus and won. However, if she seizes again, I'd like to see her."

My shoulders sagged as a weight I hadn't known I carried was lifted away. But with it, something else came to mind, making me uneasy all over again.

Ignoring the pounding of my heart, I asked the dreaded question, *"Do you need to take any more samples from me."*

Noticing the shaking in my hands, Dahlia's expression turned sympathetic. "No. We have plenty. I won't do that to you."

Kaden wrapped his arm around my shoulders and

pulled me to his chest. I could tell from his expression that he was beginning to agree with me. He didn't want Mason to stay any more than I did, but this was his place. Mason would regret it, and maybe eventually resent us if he didn't stay.

After a deep, cleansing breath, I looked up and met Mason's gaze. Concern laced with his lingering anger made me smile sadly. I would miss him.

"Stay," I signed. *"They need you."*

"And you don't," he stated. His voice had gone monotone, and I shook my head vigorously. He was so wrong.

"I do. I need you very much. But this is where you want to be." I continued on when he began to argue. *"This isn't goodbye. I'll be waiting. I promise."* I leaned into Kaden and signed, *"We will be waiting."*

He looked so angry, I didn't think he'd want me to, but I couldn't leave without kissing him one last time.

I had to stand on my toes to reach him, and when he stood stiff and refused to meet me halfway, I changed the location of my kiss. My lips lingered on his cheek, hoping he'd give in and take my mouth hungrily, as he'd done in the past, time and time again. But he didn't. And eventually, I fell back on to my heels and turned away.

Knowing I was seconds away from breaking down, I went straight to the door, without looking back. Annabelle might have disapproved of my decision, but her arms opened wide for me, and I went into them willingly.

She wrapped her arms around my shoulders and pulled me into the hallway. Already, tears were gathering at the corners of my eyes as Kaden's goodbye floated out from behind us.

"I'll take care of her," Kaden told him. "Just come back to us soon, okay?"

"You know I don't want to stay," Mason said, his voice harsh.

"Yes, you do." Seconds later, Kaden stepped out of the room, his grim face brightening slightly when he looked at me. "Ready?" he asked.

Though it felt like I was leaving a piece of me behind, I took a deep breath and reminded myself it was the right thing to do. I'd done a lot of selfish things over the months since I'd met Mason and Kaden, and now I had a chance to make things right.

Nodding my acceptance, I clutched Kaden's hand, ready to get home, put this whole nightmare behind me, and start a life Mason would be proud to come home to.

"Fuck this," Mason shouted. "Jane!"

We all stopped as Mason burst from the room, his face hard and determined as he came straight for me. Without preamble, he gripped my face in his hands and kissed me. Panic and desperation laced the kiss, and all I could do was grip his shoulders and hold on as tightly as I could as it spun out of control.

I didn't realize I was crying until the kiss slowed down enough to feel his thumbs gently wiping the tears from my cheeks. How was I going to leave him?

When Mason pulled away, his own eyes were watery, which brought on another wave of tears. Sniffing, I tried to step out of his arms. It was too hard to be so close to him.

"No, don't leave me," he begged.

"*I have to,*" I signed. "*I can't be selfish this time.*"

I was suddenly smashed against his chest, his arms like a vice around my back. I should have tried to pull away, but my willpower had depleted. Instead, I pressed my face against his shirt and took a deep breath, committing his scent to memory.

His warm breath tickled my ear, and I shivered. "Let me be the selfish one this time."

He let me lean back so I could look him in the eyes.

"They don't need me," he said. "Most of it's in your head. And that's my fault. I left you, without much warning, thinking I could make a difference. And I have. But it's over now."

I shook my head in denial. Dahlia had said she could use his help. I looked over Mason's shoulder to see her standing at the door, but I couldn't read her expression.

Reading my thoughts, Mason pressed his lips to my cheek. "She wants my help, but it's not necessary. And it wouldn't matter anyway. I'm not staying," he said firmly. "I need you. And I'm making you a promise right here, right now. I promise to never leave you again."

I shook my head, no. I didn't want him making promises he couldn't keep. *Don't*, I mouthed.

Ignoring my protest, he repeated the words so vehemently, he left no room for argument or doubt that he meant it from the deepest parts of his soul. "I promise."

14

THE MORNINGS WERE BEGINNING TO GET COOLER ONCE again, but the days were still warm and fragrant with the scents of lingering summer. Arms behind my head, I laid back on the red gingham blanket under the largest oak tree on the property and closed my eyes, soaking in the last rays of afternoon sun. The tree's limbs swayed in the breeze, casting me in and out of the shadows, cooling me down before I became too hot.

It was the perfect day to lay about. We'd been home for nearly three months, and every moment of that time had been spent getting our little farm up to par. Annabelle and I had done a lot of work when we'd first found the place, but there was still so much more to do.

We cleaned up the vegetable gardens, made them bigger, and fixed the barn and animal pens out back. Annabelle and I had ignored that section of the property before, but now we had plans to find livestock.

The bleat of a goat in the distance made me smile and reminded me that we did house one creature already. A demanding goat who wanted attention every chance she got.

I was hoping to add a dog into the mix as well. If we ever ran across one as sweet as Poco. My grin slipped, remembering the crazy dog. I missed him. Along with Annabelle and Aidan, who I was just getting to know well. After checking on Naahir's old compound, they'd been welcomed with open arms and had decided to stay. I admitted, the place was ideal. Especially once they got rid of a few problem people.

We were offered a place to stay as well, but Kaden, Mason, and I preferred our privacy.

A light tickle on the underside of arm sent goosebumps racing across my skin. It continued up to the crease of my elbow and I couldn't take it anymore. Smiling, I rolled away, but was caught and had to endure the torture of having my ribs gently tickled.

"Open your eyes, and I'll stop," the deep voice of my attacker demanded.

At first, I resisted, but the rebellion didn't last long, as a new round of tickling began, this time at the sensitive spot above my knee.

My eyes popped open to the refreshing sight of Kaden's massive smile. Something that I'd not had the pleasure of witnessing until just recently. It had taken him some time, but once we were home and settling back into a routine, he began to relax more and more each day.

Though a cure and a vaccine had been developed, nothing drastic had changed in our little world. We still had to keep an eye on the perimeter for threats from both the living and the dead. However, we'd been incredibly lucky and had little to no problems from either.

"There she is," another voice said to my right and I turned my smile on Mason.

He tucked a strand of hair behind my ear, and I took advantage of his closeness. I grabbed his hand before he could pull it away and gave the pad of his thumb a light nip. His gasp shot sizzling desire straight to my core.

He froze, his eyes sharpening onto what I was doing to his thumb, drawing it into my mouth before slowly releasing it and moving on to the next. From the way his gaze darkened to a lovely shade of mahogany as I flicked the tip, the middle finger was the most sensitive. I leisurely slid the digit in and out, making sure to keep eye contact, showing exactly what I wanted to do to another part of his anatomy, which I could feel hardening against my thigh.

I'd wanted to playfully tease him, but somehow, I ended up turning myself on. I shifted my hips on the blanket but was restricted by Kaden's bracketing thighs at my knees. I flicked my gaze up to the patient man above me and almost choked on Mason's finger as he pushed it into my mouth. Kaden's half-lidded stare held me hostage as he watched us.

"Little minx," Mason murmured. "We were trying to give you a relaxing picnic. And here you are seducing us."

Using his free hand, he traced the dark circles under my eyes and frowned, no doubt remembering how I'd thrashed in bed the night before. The memories of my time in the facility would hit me hardest during the darkest parts of the night. But while in the arms of my lovers, even the worst of my nightmares were beginning to fade. And when they did consume me, I did my best to hide them. Especially from Mason.

He'd kept his promise to me and hadn't left my side

for more than a few hours at a time. I'd told him over and over again that I never took his promise so literally, but he still suffered from needless guilt.

The three of us were healing from our rocky start. I forgave and had been forgiven. The moment we'd climbed out of that cave, we began making our trek home and towards our fresh start. No more blame, lies, or apologies. Just us, together, building the life we all three craved.

Mason pushed another finger into my mouth, a little harder this time, lighting me on fire.

"Suck," he said, all playfulness gone from his tone.

No longer was I the one in control. Or maybe I never had been. And maybe I liked it better this way. I sucked hard on the digits earning me a deep groan for my efforts.

"Stay there", he said, slipping his fingers out of my mouth.

I would have protested, but he sat back on his knees and began unbuckling his leather belt. My palms landed on Kaden's hard thighs, my excitement so strong I dug my fingers into the denim of his pants.

Kaden pulled one of my hands away from his thigh and pressed it again his arousal hardening beneath his jeans. A rumble rose from his chest as I rubbed the length up to the tip and back down.

"Enough," he growled, pressing down on my hand. He leaned over me, blocking my view of Mason to kiss me.

It wasn't a light or teasing kiss. His lips moved over mine, hard and fierce. I shivered, opening my mouth to his hot tongue, and my world tilted.

He suddenly broke the kiss and whispered, "I want you." There was a question there, but it was unnecessary.

He owned me. He had from the moment I'd met him. They both had.

He looked down as I signed between us, *"I want you, too."*

"I'm yours," he said, taking my mouth once more, hard and fast, before breaking away to slide down my body.

"Take this off," he demanded, tugging at my shirt. He helped me strip both my shirt and my bra before pulling at the elastic of my leggings. "These, too." But this time, I didn't get a chance to help. He pulled them down swiftly, taking my socks with them.

I reached for my underwear, but he stopped me. "Leave them." I raised an eyebrow at the demand, but he gave me nothing but a wicked smile that left me breathless.

"God, you're gorgeous," Mason said, catching my attention.

He knelt next to me, completely naked, his cock only inches from my lips. I licked them in anticipation, then couldn't contain myself. I wrapped a hand around his warm arousal, loving the moan he let slip as I teased the tip with a swipe of my thumb.

My attention was suddenly split again when Kaden's lips wrapped around my nipple, hot and moist. He sucked hard, the small ache of pleasure making me gasp. He moved to the other nipple, and I lost my train of thought. It wasn't until he began to trail wet kisses down my torso that I remembered what I'd been doing, and gave Mason a squeeze.

"Take me in your mouth, Sweetheart," Mason croaked. "Before I start begging."

Grinning, I opened my mouth, eager to accept him.

He moaned and I swallowed, taking him almost all the way into my mouth. He thrust in and out, gazing down at me with lust and love.

"So gorgeous," he said, trailing his fingers over my cheeks.

"I'm in total agreement." Kaden nipped at my hip, then kissed and licked a tantalizing path to my belly button that had me wiggling beneath them.

He quickly changed position and spread my legs, giving me no warning before he licked me through the cotton between my thighs. My hips jerked on their own, seeking more, but his two large hands held me down. It was almost too much, and I swore I was about to explode right then and there. Then he blew hot puffs of air against my throbbing clit, sending an uncontrollable spasm through the muscles in my stomach.

Mason paused mid-thrust. "Damn, what did you do?"

Kaden didn't answer. Instead, he ripped away my underwear and sunk two fingers inside of me. My eyes watered, and I sucked hard on Mason's cock. Unable to cry out my pleasure, I took it out on him.

Mason didn't complain. In fact, he held the back of my head and thrust hard, hitting the back of my throat. I squeezed the base of his cock, encouraging him, all the while listening closely to the sounds of Kaden taking off his jeans. He pulled away to rip open a condom wrapper. My inside clenched as a hungry heat flowed through me. I needed him, both of them inside me now.

Reading my mind, as usual, Kaden was there. He thrust inside of me just as Mason pulled out of my mouth, both giving me time to adjust. I wrapped my legs around Kaden's waist, reaching for him with my free hand. He entwined his fingers with mine, bringing them to his mouth to lick and suck just as I'd done to Mason's.

Things changed rapidly between the three of us then. The hunger that had slowly been building suddenly became frantic. We kiss, we fucked, and we made love with a passion that should have scared me. I didn't know where one of us ended and the other began. But I wanted that intensity. I couldn't get enough. And neither could they.

15

———

THE AFTERNOON SUN WAS JUST BEGINNING TO DIP TOWARDS the horizon when I finally stirred. I rolled to my side, burrowing my nose into the warm chest next to me, smiling when the owner chuckled. Whether he was laughing at me or with me, I didn't care. As long as he laughed.

Kaden brushed his lips against the top of my head and I sighed contentedly. His chest hairs tickled my cheek, and I ran my fingers through them, pulling lightly until he placed a hand over mine.

"Sleep well?" he asked.

I nodded, though he didn't need my answer. He could see it in the way my entire body relaxed. A couple of hours of dreamless sleep had been exactly what I needed.

"We can do this," Kaden murmured so softly I almost didn't catch it.

I looked up, tilting my head in question.

"Us," he answered. "We can do this. Build a life." He smiled as though just realizing it was possible. I knew how he felt, though. I fought panic attacks almost on a daily basis, worried something would go wrong. That one of us would be ripped away from here.

Feeling me tremble, Kaden rubbed soothing circles over my back. "I'm sorry," he said. "I didn't mean that to sound so depressing. I'm happy. Scared, but happy. I'm trying not to worry about the things I can't control."

His smile turned self-deprecating as he snorted. "We both need to work on that, huh?"

Couldn't argue with that.

Relaxing back into his arms, I kissed him before wiggling to get my hands free. Instead of letting me go, he tightened his arms and rolled over onto his back.

"No more talking," he said darkly, and I was suddenly aware that we were both still naked as the day we were born.

I wiggled again, this time with my lower body, rubbing all the important bits. Kaden's eyes rolled back and he groaned.

"You're going to kill me," he said. Then he rolled us quickly until he hovered over me.

Kaden's eyes twinkled down at me, and all I could do was smile back at him. At this point, I was pretty sure a smile had been permanently etched onto my face.

"Remember when we first found you, and you ran from us?" he asked.

Though my brows furrowed at the change of subject, I nodded.

"I caught up to you, and we trip over each other." He chuckled and his face turned red with embarrassment, surprising me. "I didn't mean to fall on top of you, and then my body betrayed me."

He shook his head again, but this time he was serious. "I was so afraid of scaring you, but I wanted you so badly.

It wasn't just about that fact we hadn't seen anyone, let alone another woman, in years. It was you. The moment I laid eyes on you, my frozen heart thawed. And I knew. I had to do whatever it took to take care of you. No matter how you felt about me. I would have stayed your friend."

My face must have registered my shock. Though I knew he loved me, I'd not known quite so much detail about his feelings. And truthfully, this was a lot of talking for Kaden. But I was learning, with Kaden, high emotions were what brought on his chatty side.

"Then you strolled out of that barn and stood before me. Your naked skin glowing in the moonlight. That first night will be a part of me forever."

I melted then. How could I not? The vulnerable intensity in his gaze drew my lips to his, and I kiss him with everything I felt. Expressing what I couldn't say out loud.

I licked across his bottom lip, slipping the tip just inside. He opened his mouth and our tongues entwined as our limbs began doing the same when a strange thumping sound pulled us apart.

We both stilled and listened carefully to the roaring sound of a helicopter getting closer.

"Where's Mason?" I signed, quite a bit frantically. I'd meant to ask him earlier, but he'd distracted me.

Kaden jumped to his feet and held out a hand to help up. "He's walking the fences," he said, handing me my clothes.

We both dressed quickly and ran toward the house, leaving the blanket and picnic supplies for now. I reached for Kaden's hand, and he gripped it tightly as though he too was worried we'd jinxed ourselves with our earlier conversation.

The helicopter lowered onto a small section of clear land about forty yards from the house. Mason was already there waiting. When he saw us, the panic on his face matched everything I was feeling.

"Do you know who it is?" Kaden asked.

"No."

We didn't have to wait long. The door popped open revealing a familiar face. Dahlia's wide smile was catching, and I found myself wanting to smile back. But then, a horrible thought came to mind, and my grip on Kaden's hand tightened.

"You're okay," Kaden murmured. "We're here."

At first, I was confused, but then I realized he thought I was scared they were here for me. No, that actually hadn't even occurred to me.

I shook my head at Kaden and looked at Mason. Understanding dawned on Kaden's face and he grimaced.

"Dahlia!" Mason exclaimed, rushing to meet the woman once she was cleared of the helicopter blades. The pilot, I noticed, didn't get out.

Dahlia looked pretty much the same as she had the last time I'd seen her. A backpack was thrown over her burgundy turtleneck, which was tucked into black skinny jeans. The whole outfit made her look slim and curvy all at once. Her long brown hair had been pulled into an intricate knot at the back of her head.

Feeling self-conscious, I reached up to my messy ponytail, smoothing the hairs with no success. I probably looked like I'd been rolling around on the ground all afternoon. Which was exactly what I'd been doing.

Mason gave her a short hug, and I was pleased when his touch didn't linger too long. If I hadn't been so worried she was here to steal Mason away again, I would have rolled my eyes at my jealousy.

"How are you?" Mason asked her.

"I'm good," she responded. "You?"

"Oh, we're great." He looked back and Kaden and me, his smile slipping at our dower expressions.

"Kaden, Jane," Dahlia greeted, moving towards us. "How are you?"

"Fine," Kaden replied. "I don't mean to be rude, but, what are you doing here?"

She laughed and surprisingly, even though Kaden had been extremely rude, the smile reached her eyes.

"I know you must be thinking the worst, but I promise I'm not here to cause you alarm."

"What's going on?" Mason asked, coming to stand on the other side of me. As soon as he took my free hand, I began to relax. We were a united front, ready to deal with whatever news, good or bad, Dahlia was here to deliver.

"Well, first, I wanted to check to see how Mason and Jane were doing. Especially Jane," she said. "Have there been any problems? Any more seizures?"

I shook my head no, not willing to let go of the mens' hands just yet. Dahlia glanced down at the tight grip we had on one another and her smile turned sad.

"I didn't mean to bother you," she began, but Mason interrupted her.

"You're not bothering us. But you can understand why we're wary."

"I can. Again, I'm sorry about everything. I hope one day we can be friends. All of us," she said, looking at me.

Taking a breath through my nose, I let it out slowly and nodded. I would like to be her friend. The memories were just too fresh at the moment.

"To answer your questions," Kaden said, "Jane has been fine. No seizures or other unusual side effects."

"That's good," she sighed with relief. "But again, if something does happen, let me know right away."

"Let you know?" Kaden asked slowly. "How?"

Her expression brightened as she swung her backpack over one shoulder and pulled out a small silver rectangle. She held out, but none of us reached for it.

"Well, don't just stare at it. Here." She thrust the cell phone into Kaden's hand. With a press of his thumb, the screen lit up.

"Towers are coming back online. And I made sure you were one of the first to get service," she told us. "I also programmed my number along with Annabelle and Aidan's."

At my surprised look, she smiled. "I've already been by to see my brother. Annabelle will be calling you shortly, I'm sure. She seemed excited to finally be able to talk to you every day. Or text, in your case."

I smiled, shaking my head. But deep down I felt the same way as my friend. I missed her.

"Internet isn't up quite yet. But it's coming," Dahlia announced, sending another shockwave through us. "And before you ask," she said, pointing to the house. We all turned to see a yellow glow coming from within. "It's not perfect, so expect outages every once in a while. Things are progressing fast now. We still have a lot of work to do, but we're getting there."

When the three of us stood stunned, she laughed and began walking towards the helicopter.

"Hey, where are you going?" Mason called.

"I can't stay," she said. "I have a few more stops to

make and a meeting with the President in two hours. But don't worry. We'll talk soon!"

A few moments later, she was gone, and the three of us were left staring at one another.

She was right; the power was back on. A little weak, but still incredible. We'd had limited use of electricity by using generators, but this was different. The hum of electricity was surprisingly loud when we walked into the house.

A buzzing noise made me jump. Kaden had set the cell phone on the table, and it vibrated against the wood noisily. At first, I just stared, then with a roll of my eyes, I scooped it up and looked at the screen, smiling when I saw Aidan's name. Though I instinctively knew it wasn't Aidan texting.

OMG Jane! Can you believe this?

It's incredible, I texted back

Right!? Things are going back to normal.

Normal… I glanced back at Kaden and Mason, who watched me, love and lust written all over their faces. *Our* normal sounded good. Whatever that was, I looked forward to finding out.

16

THE NEXT NIGHT, THE TEMPERATURE DROPPED, ENOUGH TO light the logs in the fireplace for the first time since we'd been back. I curled up in Mason's lap on the couch with a sigh. Still not used to having limitless electricity, we hadn't turned on the lamps and instead, let the flames light up the shadows.

Warm against Mason's chest, I was content and just on the verge of falling asleep when Kaden walked into the room carrying a guitar.

I sat up, no longer sleepy. *"Where'd you get that?"* I signed.

"I found it a while back." He looked up at me, his gaze shining at me from the flickering flames. "I'm probably kind of rusty, but do you mind if I play?"

I shook my head no, and he sat down in the chair opposite of us.

"You're in for a treat," Mason whispered in my ear. He wrapped his arms around me and pulled me back until I relaxed into him. "He hasn't played in a long time, but you've heard him sing. He's amazing."

I had heard him sing. Just the one time. The night we first made love, Kaden had drawn me out of that run-down barn with his achingly deep voice. He hadn't sung to me since, and I'd been too much of a coward to ask for an encore.

Kaden plucked the first note, and like magic, he had me again. I rested my head on Mason's shoulder as Kaden sang to us a song I'd never heard before. It wasn't long until I realized he had to have written it. Because it was the story of us. Of how we fell into each other. How we loved and lost. And how we began again.

The End

C.E. BLACK

is a Maggie Award Winning Author in Paranormal Romance. She self-published her first book in 2011 and has since published several novels, novellas, and short stories in the Paranormal, Fantasy, and Sci-Fi Romance genres. Though steamy romance, hunky heroes, and feisty heroines are C.E.'s specialty, she enjoys surprising her readers with action-filled plots and exciting twists that make for a fast-paced read.

Her official website is www.ceblack.org.